"How did you find me?"

"We got a tip that you were at the clinic with a newborn. Bear and I followed you from there."

"So did my former fiancé," Violet muttered. "You should have put your time into tracking him down instead."

"We have troopers waiting at the park entrance where I found his abandoned car. If he returns there, he'll walk right into them. Making sure you and your baby were safe was my priority. There's a blizzard blowing in, and you have a newborn."

"I'm very aware of that fact," she said, sidling past Gabe and moving away from the door. "But we'd have been fine. I know how to take care of myself and my daughter."

"I'm sure you do, but Bear and I plan on helping in any way we can."

ALASKA K-9 UNIT

*These state troopers fight for justice
with the help of their brave canine partners.*

Alaskan Rescue by Terri Reed
Wilderness Defender by Maggie K. Black
Undercover Mission by Sharon Dunn
Tracking Stolen Secrets by Laura Scott
Deadly Cargo by Jodie Bailey
Arctic Witness by Heather Woodhaven
Yukon Justice by Dana Mentink
Blizzard Showdown by Shirlee McCoy
Christmas K-9 Protectors by Lenora Worth and Maggie K. Black

Aside from her faith and her family, there's not much **Shirlee McCoy** enjoys more than a good book! When she's not hanging out with the people she loves most, she can be found plotting her next Love Inspired Suspense story or trekking through the wilderness, training with a local search-and-rescue team. Shirlee loves to hear from readers. If you have time, drop her a line at shirleermccoy@hotmail.com.

Books by Shirlee McCoy

Love Inspired Suspense

Hidden Witness
Evidence of Innocence

FBI: Special Crimes Unit

Night Stalker
Gone
Dangerous Sanctuary
Lone Witness
Falsely Accused

Alaska K-9 Unit

Blizzard Showdown

Visit the Author Profile page at LoveInspired.com for more titles.

BLIZZARD SHOWDOWN

SHIRLEE McCOY

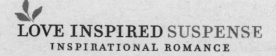

LOVE INSPIRED SUSPENSE
INSPIRATIONAL ROMANCE

Special thanks and acknowledgment are given to Shirlee McCoy for her contribution to the Alaska K-9 Unit miniseries.

LOVE INSPIRED® SUSPENSE

INSPIRATIONAL ROMANCE

Recycling programs for this product may not exist in your area.

ISBN-13: 978-1-335-55467-3

Blizzard Showdown

Love Inspired
22 Adelaide St. West, 40th Floor
Toronto, Ontario M5H 4E3, Canada
www.LoveInspired.com

Printed in U.S.A.

But ask now the beasts, and they shall teach thee;
and the fowls of the air, and they shall tell thee:
Or speak to the earth, and it shall teach thee:
and the fishes of the sea shall declare unto thee.
Who knoweth not in all these that the hand of the Lord
hath wrought this? In whose hand is the soul of
every living thing, and the breath of all mankind.
—*Job* 12:7-10

To the members of Chesapeake Search Dogs
who volunteer their time and resources to bring home the
lost and missing, and to search-and-rescue professionals
everywhere who selflessly give so that others might live.
You are wonderful examples of what sacrificial love
looks like. May He guide and protect your efforts
and multiply your strengths.

ONE

Violet James didn't want to step outside.

Not because of the cold wind that beat against the windows of the medical clinic. Not even because she had her newborn daughter strapped to her chest.

She didn't want to go outside because she was terrified.

Even now, after seven months of hiding in the Alaskan outback, she wasn't safe. She would never be. Not unless the police caught her former fiancé, Lance Wells, and tossed him in jail where he belonged.

She shuddered, trying not to picture his handsome face or remember his crooning voice and sweet promises. She'd believed every word he'd said. All the I-love-yous and the forever-afters.

She'd been a fool, and it had almost cost her best friend, Ariel Potter, her life. It *had* cost the wilderness guide Violet had hired his. Violet had been planning a small wedding. Just her best friend and Lance's. The guide, Cal Brooks, was going to take them into Alaska's pristine wilderness for a weeklong adventure. When they returned, they'd exchange vows at a beautiful little cabin on Eklutna Lake.

Instead, the guide had been murdered.

Ariel had been pushed off a cliff.

And Violet had run for her life.

She didn't like remembering that day.

The helplessness she'd felt when she'd discovered Cal's body, blood pooling beneath his torso, still sent chills down her spine. She'd tried to render aid, calling for help and hoping someone in the wedding party would hear her. But there'd been no one else around in the vast expanse of Chugach State Park. After she and Lance had gotten engaged, she'd set the wedding date in April and had rented two cabins as far away from the bright lights of Anchorage as she could get. She'd thought it would be romantic...that they'd create unforgettable memories.

Her memories were unforgettable, but not for the reason she had hoped. Instead of following through with her plans to exchange vows with the guy of her dreams, she had found herself fleeing from the man of her nightmares.

She had made *so* many mistakes. Missed so many red flags. She hadn't had a chance to talk to Ariel about it. But she knew what her best friend would say: *Give yourself a break. You couldn't have known*.

Maybe not.

She liked to think she had not been blinded by love. That she had gone into the engagement the same way she went into business meetings—clear-headed and focused.

The truth was, she had been swept away by her deep

need for connection and family. She had allowed herself to be blind to Lance's less-than-desirable personality traits because she had craved closeness and had been tired of being alone.

She had been desperate for family after her parents' deaths.

Lance had offered her a chance to, once again, be part of a loving home. He had known all the right things to say to make her mourning heart feel joy again.

And she had bought into it.

Even when he had balked at the idea of signing pre-nups. Even when he had asked her to change the way she dressed and the way she wore her hair. Even when every sign pointed to the fact that he wasn't ever going to love anyone as much as he loved himself, she had allowed herself to believe the lies he'd told her.

She had wanted family so much that she had been willing to compromise on things that she shouldn't have. Like the vacation home in Florida—a multimillion-dollar property that Lance had made a cash offer on.

Her cash, of course.

The plan had been to fly to Florida after their wedding, complete the purchase and then honeymoon in their dream vacation home.

Only it hadn't been her dream.

It had been his.

She had been the bankroll, paying his way.

Despite the bragging he had done about the small business he owned, he never seemed to have money. After the first few months of their relationship, when I-love-yous had been exchanged and the future was being planned, he had stopped paying for dinners and trips.

She had paid for their dates, fueled their cars and told herself that it was all perfectly normal.

She had known it wasn't.

Deep in her heart, she had understood that something was very wrong with her relationship. She just hadn't been able to admit it.

When he had insisted they put the money for the Florida property in a joint account, she'd balked, but he'd hounded her about it, accusing her of selfishness and arrogance, until she'd complied.

He had been a master manipulator.

She only wished that she had realized that before they had gone to the bank together and opened a new account. She had transferred two million dollars of the money she had inherited from her parents.

Lance had been thrilled. He'd treated her to a lovely dinner. Praised her beauty. And told her they would spend the rest of their lives together, splitting time between Anchorage and Miami. Then, later that night, he had given her a diamond bracelet to wear on their wedding day. She should have been charmed, but she'd noticed that the money had come from the account they'd just opened. She'd been embarrassed for him and for her. She would rather he have given her a card with something lovely written inside than an expensive gift that she had paid for.

That night, she'd transferred the house money back into her account, leaving nothing but a few thousand dollars.

She hadn't told him.

If she hadn't been pregnant, she probably would have ended the relationship. But there'd been a baby to think about. An unexpected complication to a relationship that had already gone from romance-of-the-century to having her question whether her groom-to-be had ever truly loved her. She hadn't told Lance she was pregnant. She had been worried about his reaction.

That should have been another huge clue to the fact that he wasn't the right person for her.

She frowned, staring out into the bright sunlight, wishing she had made dozens of different choices.

She didn't regret having her daughter, but she regretted the decisions she'd made that led her here—a medical clinic on the edge of Anchorage, desperate, scared and on the run from Lance *and* the police.

"Are you okay, hon?" a receptionist asked.

"Fine," Violet said, shoving open the door and stepping outside without looking back.

She couldn't afford to make a spectacle of herself.

Even sleep-deprived and ever more anxious to return to civilization, she had to make decisions that would protect her baby and protect the survivalist family who had taken her in and helped her stay hidden for the past seven months.

The Seavers lived off the grid in Chugach State Park. Violet had learned a lot from them, but she didn't want to raise her daughter in an underground bunker in the wilderness. She wanted to bring Ava home to the beautiful house she had grown up in and offer her little girl the same security and sense of belonging she had felt growing up.

"We'll get back there, sweetie," she murmured, patting the baby's back as she hurried along the sidewalk. Brisk October air stung her cheeks and ruffled her hair.

She pulled her hood up, more to cover her face than to keep her warm.

Violet wore a dark wig and heavy makeup, thick glasses and layers of clothes, but despite her meticulous disguise, she still worried that Lance would find her. If he did, she knew he wouldn't hesitate to kill her. She had no idea what he would do to their daughter, and that scared her more than anything.

She touched Ava's back, feeling for the subtle rise and fall. At just a few weeks preterm, her daughter had arrived during the first major storm of the season. Labor had been quick and brutal, over almost before Violet had processed the fact that it had begun.

Dana Seaver, the matriarch of the family, had helped her through the birth. It certainly hadn't been the kind of labor Violet had planned or imagined. She had thought she would be at the medical clinic where she had been going for prenatal care, with doctors, midwives and nurses available during labor.

Instead, Ava had been born in an underground bunker. All the necessary things had been sterilized, but that didn't change the fact that the walls were packed earth, lined with shelves that contained all the supplies the Seaver family would need for the winter.

There had been no natural light. Oil lamps had illuminated the birthing area Dana had created once she had realized there would be no time to get Violet to the hospital.

If things had gone wrong…

But, fortunately, they hadn't.

One of the things Violet had been trying to learn during her exile was that dwelling on the past did nothing to change the present or the future.

That would be easier to do once Lance was in prison.

And when the authorities finally apprehended him, she planned to turn herself in to the Anchorage police department, tell her side of the story so she could clear her name and then finally move on with her life.

Please, God, let it be soon.

Bright sunlight reflected off the pavement and flashed on the windshields of passing vehicles, hiding the drivers from view. That made her nervous. Anyone could be driving past.

If Lance did, would he recognize her? She knew that was a long shot because of her disguise, but still, she couldn't afford to let her guard down. Or take their safety for granted. As always, keeping Ava away from her father was foremost in Violet's mind.

She walked across another street, forcing herself not to rush. She had to act as if she had all the time in the world. A woman with no worries…with no one hunting her. A mother and child out enjoying a beautiful fall day.

There were storm clouds in the distance, hovering over the mountains and threatening to bring snow showers and heavy winds. The Seavers listened to the weather report religiously, always prepping for the next change in the forecast. Cold weather was coming, and they had spent the past few months preparing. Violet had helped as much as she could, understanding that her presence had strained the survivalists' resources. Ava's birth had added to the burden. The family needed more of everything to sustain the two lives they had added to their fold.

One day, when this was all over and she was home with her daughter, Violet would find a way to repay them for all they had done.

She passed several shops, glancing into the windows, pretending to look at parkas and coats, clothing and fishing gear. In reality, she was studying the people behind her.

She had learned to be careful without being obvious about it.

Seven months on the run did that to a person.

She turned onto the road that led out of town. The trailhead wasn't far away, and she felt confident in her ability to find it and then find her way back to the bunker. It had taken months to get to that point. Up until recently, she had always been accompanied by one of the Seavers—usually Harrison, the Seavers' teenage son. Sometimes Cole. Father and son were confident in the wilds of Alaska and comfortable in urbanized settings. Dana preferred to stay close to home, tending herb and produce gardens in greenhouses she'd built far off the beaten paths.

The family would have been happy to let Violet stay in their quiet sanctuary forever, but even though Violet had never been the social butterfly the press had painted her to be, she missed all the trappings of civilization. She liked going to the grocery store when she needed food or supplies. She enjoyed seeing other people when she was out shopping. She had no desire to spend hours making candles or heating water to wash clothes in deep tubs.

She wanted what she'd had before she had met Lance—
a quiet life filled with the people she loved and admired.

At long last she reached the edge of a neighborhood
that abutted the park. The sky had darkened, wispy
white clouds gathering into steel-gray masses. Soon
the storm would hit. She wanted to be back at the bunker by then. She *needed* to be. As terrifying as Lance
was, the Alaskan bush during a blizzard was even more
terrifying.

Suddenly, a car engine revved, the driver acceler-
ated off a side road and appeared to be heading straight
for Violet.

Lance!

It had to be!

Shocked, she jumped sideways, stumbling behind a
hedge grove between two properties. The driver braked
hard, barely missing a vehicle parked on the curb, then
backed up and sped forward again.

She ran around the side of a house, flying across the
yard and into the woods behind it. As she sprinted between sparse trees, the sound of a slamming car door
filling her with dread. Her wig caught on a branch and
was yanked from her head. She left it there, every cell
in her body focused on escape. One hand cupping the
delicate curve of Ava's skull, the other shoving aside
leaves as she raced headlong into the park, she prayed
that somehow, *someway* she could outrun the man who
wanted her dead.

The first flakes of snow fell as Gabriel Runyon got
out of his vehicle. They splattered on his cheeks and

melted, icy rivulets running into the open collar of his coat. He pulled up his hood and grabbed his emergency pack. Dry clothes. Material for building a shelter. Fire starters. Food for Bear. Water. Energy bars. Enough to keep him and his K-9 partner going for a few days. *If* the weather didn't worsen.

He glanced at the darkening sky. The meteorologists were calling for a blizzard. If that happened, and he and Bear were stranded, they could survive, but could a woman who who had just given birth?

Could a newborn baby?

He, along with members of his Alaskan K-9 unit, had spent the last seven months trying to locate Violet James, Lance Wells and Jared Dennis. They were all wanted for questioning in the murder of a wilderness guide and the attempted murder of Ariel Potter— a woman who had been pushed off a cliff and left for dead. He and the K-9 team had followed tracks through the Alaskan wilderness, visited every medical clinic and hospital in Anchorage, and spent hours following up on leads. They had even reached out to church groups and charities, hoping that Violet would eventually make an appearance and that Lance would make a mistake.

There'd been sightings, calls from concerned citizens that came in a little too late, near misses that had given him hope that he was on the right track. But today had been different. He'd been following an anonymous tip that a woman named Violet James had a newborn baby and was at Helping Hands Christian Medical Clinic at the southwestern edge of Anchorage. Gabriel hadn't expected to find his quarry there, but he had followed up on the lead, arriving just in time to see a dark-haired woman step outside.

Violet had blond hair.

He had pored over photos of her. He knew she was small-framed, thin and delicate-looking. Not the sort of woman he would have expected to survive seven months alone. She'd been pampered as a child, raised by parents who had enough money to lavish her with every luxury.

He knew nothing about that lifestyle.

Gabriel had been orphaned at seven, tossed into the foster system and raised by a series of apathetic foster parents. He had no resentment about that, but he certainly had no clue what childhood stability and comfort looked like.

What he did know was that people raised with plenty often struggled when they didn't have enough. In the past several months, Violet James hadn't accessed her bank accounts or used her cell phone. She hadn't logged on to social media. So, aside from a letter she'd sent to her best friend last April, claiming her innocence in the murder of a wilderness tour guide and attempted murder of Ariel, Violet had stayed off the radar.

Had she suddenly reappeared?

Gabriel had kept his distance from the dark-haired woman, inching through midmorning traffic, his unmarked SUV helping him blend with morning commuters traveling to jobs in the center of the city. He'd lost sight of her when she'd turned down a one-way street, and by the time he'd followed the grid-like pattern of traffic onto the side road, she was gone.

As near as he could tell, she had disappeared into the Chugach State Park.

Someone had followed her.

He had flagged tire tread marks leading into shrubbery across from the park entrance. A dark sedan was abandoned there, tires stuck deep in muddy earth. Gabriel had called it in.

Now, he was going hunting.

"Ready, Bear?" he asked as he opened the back hatch.

His K-9 partner lumbered to the ground—one giant step for the St. Bernard. Trained in avalanche rescue, Bear could find a needle in a haystack. He loved cold weather, snow and the hunt. For him, this was a game, the prize a few rousing games of tug.

"I'll take that as a yes," Gabriel murmured as he pulled a search vest over Bear's boxy head. The St. Bernard stood still as Gabriel snapped straps and slid a glow stick into a pocket on the back. Night fell quickly this time of year. They both needed to be prepared.

He attached a lead to Bear's collar, called in their location again and walked into the park. A dusting of snow covered the ground. No footprints visible. Or obvious track marks.

He allowed Bear to sniff the area.

"Ready, Bear? Go find!" he called.

The K-9 took off, trotting through sparsely forested land and out onto a trail. Chugach State Park covered 495,000 acres of pristine wilderness. Even after decades of exploration, Gabriel respected the vastness and the biodiversity. Lakes. Rivers. Streams. Mountains. Forests and plains.

There was a little of everything in Chugach, and a lot of danger for the foolhardy. It would be easy for someone who didn't know the area to get lost. From what he had learned about Violet, while she had been off the grid for seven months, living in the Alaskan wilds alone didn't seem feasible for someone with her background.

Bear veered to the right, crossing a stream and bounding up a hill. Snow swirled through the shadowy forest, coating the ground in glistening white. Gabriel didn't think they were far behind their quarry. Bear's tail was high, his head up. He knew the game, and he loved it. He could go for hours if necessary.

Bear stopped as he crested the hill, snuffled the ground and raised his head to the air. His nose twitched, and then he growled.

Seconds later, a shot rang out. A bullet whizzed past, slamming into the ground a yard or so from Gabriel's feet. A warning shot meant to drive him back

He dived behind a tree, shouting for Bear to drop. The dog obeyed immediately, dropping down in an emergency stay that would hold him in place until Gabriel gave the release command.

"Alaska State Police! Drop your weapon! Now!" he called, even though he knew the perpetrator would refuse the command. Out of visual field and completely hidden, his quarry had the advantage.

For now.

Backup would be arriving shortly, but Gabriel didn't want to waste time. He crawled along the forest floor, keeping ground cover between himself and the gunman as he attempted to take a higher position. Uphill, through dense undergrowth and then along a ridge, he headed in the direction the gunshot had come from. His trek became more challenging as the wind picked up, branches bowing and swaying as snow continued to fall, but he stayed the course.

He finally reached the top of the hill and waited, listening for the sound of approach or retreat. It took just moments. Branches broke and pebbles skittered along the rock face on the far side of the hill. The perp was on the run, probably heading back to the park entrance, using the trail that wound along the top of the hill.

Gabriel followed, whistling for Bear to heel.

They moved together, pressing through the trees and stepping onto the trail. He spotted footprints in the snow. Larger ones heading west toward the trailhead and smaller ones heading east, deeper into the park. His fellow K-9 officers were heading for the park entrance. They could apprehend the shooter. He wanted to follow the smaller prints. After all these months, it was time to finally meet Violet James face-to-face and get her side of the story of how a wilderness guide had ended up dead and her best friend at the bottom of a cliff.

He turned east, following the footprints across the crest of the hill and down the nose. The trail meandered along a clear stream that gurgled over smooth rocks. The footprints veered in that direction, leading to the bank of the river, deep prints in the muddy shoreline. Then nothing.

Whoever it was didn't want to be followed and was making it as difficult as possible.

That was fine.

Gabriel liked a challenge, and he had no intention of giving up before he found his prey.

"Bear! Find!" he commanded.

Bear loped into the water, splashing to the opposite shore, his head to the wind as he darted away from the safety of the trail and deep into the Alaskan wilderness.

TWO

The temperature was falling, snow pouring from the sky. Daylight had turned dusky with storm clouds. Even dressed for the weather, which she was, a person could only survive so long outside in conditions like these.

Swirling snow was creating whiteout conditions, and she didn't dare travel through the park without a good visual of the surroundings.

Violet shoved through thick foliage, Ava's warm body pressed against her chest and tucked carefully beneath her parka. She had heard a gunshot a while ago. Since then, there'd been nothing but the rushing sound of the river, the babble of brooks and the soft sigh of wind through the trees. She picked her way up steep drainage, careful not to slip on the snow-coated rocks as she laser focused on what she needed to do.

Get to shelter.

Build a fire.

Wait the storm out.

Return to the bunker.

Go back into hiding until Ava's next well-baby checkup.

Repeat it all again.

Ava wiggled against her chest, letting out a quiet mewl and reminding Violet that she hadn't nursed since they had left the bunker that morning.

"It's okay, sweetie," she murmured, patting Ava's back as she crested the hill. She stood at the top, looking for some clue as to where she was and where she needed to go to reach safety. Everything looked the same. Trees. Deadfall. Ground cover. All blanketed with white. The forest had gone eerily quiet. No crunch of deer hooves on leaves or rustle of vixens readying their dens for spring litters.

She was alone, and she felt it. All the animals had gone to ground as they waited for the storm to pass, and she was standing on a hill, being blasted by arctic wind, a helpless newborn in her arms.

Her heart thumped heavily against her ribs, her pulse racing as adrenaline poured through her. It had been a while since she'd been this afraid and this certain that she would be lost forever in the wilderness.

"Calm down," she snapped. "Panicking will get you nowhere. Look around. You know this area. You've hiked it dozens of times looking for berries and mushrooms. You've fished in the river right below this hill."

She blew out a breath. Unless she missed her guess, Lance had given up chasing her as soon as she had left the trail. Her former fiancé had never been an outdoorsy type and had conceded going on a guided wilderness adventure only because she had wanted it so badly. At the time, she had thought he was trying to please her because he loved her. He had convinced her that he would always put her needs first, sacrificing his own desires to make her happy. In truth, the only needs he had cared about were his own. He'd wanted her money. Plain and simple. He would have done anything to get it.

Knowing she had to keep moving or freeze, Violet continued on, stumbling over deadfall, one hand pressed to Ava's back, the other pushing branches out of the way. She struggled forward, shivering, legs nearly numb. She needed to get inside and warm up, but snow fell like a shroud, blinding her. Pausing, she listened for the river. Just the way Harrison had taught her.

Follow the sound of the river. Then walk along it. There are dozens of little cabins tucked along the shoreline. You never have to spend the night in the forest without shelter as long as you can make it to the river.

The storm drowned out sound, the whipping wind and whistling through the treetops mixing with the groan of old spruce trees bowing beneath the onslaught.

"God, please. Protect me and my daughter," she prayed, snow pelting her face and flying into her eyes. She thought she heard the gurgle of water over stones and headed in that direction, hoping with every fiber of her being that there was a cabin at the base of the hill.

Every hill looked alike in the wilderness.

Every tree was one of millions.

People got lost. They disappeared. Often, they were never found again.

She shuddered, forcing her mind away from the gruesome thought as she scanned the area, probing the white cloud of snow that surrounded her. Something dark rose up in front of her. There and gone as the wind shifted and the snowfall increased.

She moved toward it, nearly falling in her haste.

Ava was whimpering.

Soon she would be squalling, the sound certain to draw any hungry predators. Somewhere in the distance, a dog barked, the sound making the hair on the back of her neck stand up. There were wolves in the park, but she'd only heard them howling at night. This time of day, a barking dog almost always meant there were people nearby. On a day like today, the only people she could imagine wandering through the wilderness were police officers and first responders.

She shivered. She'd been hiding for a long time, terrified of turning herself in to the police. What would they do if they found her? Would they question and release her? Would they take her to prison for eluding them for so long and take her daughter away?

The thought terrified her.

The wind shifted again, and the cabin was in front of her. Dark stone walls. Trees pressed in close. She hurried to the front door, used the lock pick Harrison had given her to unlock it and stepped inside. The windows shuddered beneath the onslaught of the storm, the wind pushing against the door as she closed it. The Seavers, and survivalists like them, left canned goods and supplies in abandoned buildings all over the park. A failsafe that ensured survival if they were ever surprised by a storm and unable to get back home.

That would serve Violet well.

But dare she light a fire? She hesitated, rubbing Ava's back as she considered her options. There were blankets in a small chest. Dry clothes. But even with those things, the interior of the cabin was below freezing, wind seeping in through cracks in the log walls and through the thin panes of the windows.

If someone was wandering around with the dog she'd heard, she didn't want a smoke plume from the chimney to draw him to her hiding place.

On the other hand, she didn't want her baby girl to freeze.

She glanced out the window. The snow was falling faster, sheets of it limiting visibility. If anyone was out in the storm, they wouldn't last long.

Shuddering, she hurried to the fireplace and snatched up a log from a stack of wood nearby. There were matches and Vaseline-soaked cotton balls in tins on a shelf above the mantel. She grabbed both, knelt beside the hearth and prepped the fire.

The door burst inward.

Shrieking, she pivoted around, her hand cupping Ava's head, her heart hammering against her ribs. She expected to see Lance striding toward her.

Instead, a large animal barreled inside.

A *bear*?

She shrieked again, scrambling to her feet and grabbing a long piece of wood from the pile, ready to swing at the beast's head.

It stopped a few feet away, dropping onto its belly, like a...

Dog?

"He won't hurt you," a man said. "So how about you drop the wood?"

She jerked her gaze away from the giant dog.

A man stood in the doorway, his broad shoulders blocking the grayish light. He wore a dark blue coat and heavy cargo-style pants. A hat. Gloves. And winter boots made for hiking back trails.

"How about you tell me who you are and why you're in my cabin first?" she responded, her voice shaking.

She was terrified, but she didn't want him to know it.

There was a back door. If she could get to it, she could escape.

Out into the storm and the cold.

But better to be out in a blizzard alive than to be dead in a cabin. She didn't think or plan. Instead, she'd acted, swinging the wood back and tossing it at him with as much strength as she could muster.

Violet didn't wait to see where it landed.

She ran through a small doorway in the back wall, into a room that had once been sleeping quarters. Abandoned cots and shelves filled with bottles and jars of canned goods surrounded her. Too bad she didn't have time to grab blankets from the old chest.

She had barely reached the back door, her hands fumbling to lift the bar that held it closed, when her parka was snagged and she was pulled back.

She whirled, ready to fight.

Determined to free herself and her baby.

She had fought too hard to stay safe during her pregnancy to let herself be taken down now.

Violet swung a fist at Gabriel's face, but she was a foot shorter, her reach limited.

He stepped back, avoiding the first punch and grabbing her arm when she lunged at him again.

"How about we not play this game?" he suggested, Bear growling softly beside him.

"It's not a game," she snapped. "Back away and leave me alone."

"So you can go out into the storm with a newborn in your arms? I can't let you do that, Violet."

"How do you know my name?" she asked, her free hand cupping the head of the tiniest baby Gabe had ever seen.

"I'm Gabriel Runyon, a state trooper with the Alaskan K-9 unit. We've been looking for you for seven months." He fished out his badge.

She studied it for a moment, a small frown line marring the smooth skin of her forehead. "How did you find me?"

"We got a tip that you were at the clinic with a newborn. Bear and I followed you from there."

"So did my former fiancé," she muttered, her hand still on the baby's head. "You should have put your time into tracking him down instead."

"We have troopers waiting at the park entrance where I found his abandoned car. If Lance returns there, he'll be captured. Making sure you and your baby were safe was my first priority. There's a blizzard blowing in, and you have a newborn."

"I'm very aware of that fact," she said, sidling past him and moving away from the door. Cold air was blowing in through cracks in the log walls, and the door shuddered beneath the onslaught of howling wind. "But we'd have been fine. I know how to take care of myself and my daughter."

"I'm sure you do, but Bear and I plan on helping in any way we can."

"Bear?" She led the way into the main room, grabbing a log from a small stack near the fireplace and placing one in the hearth. The baby was mewling, the sound catching Bear's attention.

"My partner." He gestured in the St. Bernard's direction. Bear had his head cocked, his brown eyes focused on Violet. He was obviously curious about the noises the baby was making.

"He's…big," she said, picking up a few cotton balls that had fallen on the floor. She tossed them into the fireplace, shoved some dry kindling under the log she'd thrown into the hearth, then used flint to spark a flame.

It burned bright for a moment. Then died.

She sighed, dropping to her knees, the baby's mewls turning to a full-out cry as Violet struck the flint again.

"How about I take care of the fire and you take care of the baby?" Gabe suggested.

"I can do both," she insisted, but she didn't protest when he took the flint from her hand.

He sparked another flame, blowing gently so that it caught dry kindling. It didn't take long to get a decent fire going. That was the good news.

The bad news was that the plume of smoke rising from the chimney could attract unwanted attention.

He'd need to be vigilant until backup arrived.

By the sound of the wind and the fury of the storm, the team might not be able to make it out until dawn.

For now, they were safe.

Bear huffed quietly and settled down in front of the fire, his fur still glistening with melted snow. He rested his head on his paws, his gaze on Violet. He'd had good manners trained into him, but Gabe knew he wanted to go take a look at the crying creature Violet was holding.

"I don't think your dog likes me," Violet said uneasily. She stood a few feet away, still in her outdoor gear. Heavy parka. Small pack. The baby bundled up and held in a sling near her chest.

"He's curious about the baby. I don't think he's ever been around an infant," he responded, hoping to put her at ease. He had some questions he wanted to ask. Some things that he wanted to clarify. When Lance Wells had called 911 to report a shooting, he had told the responding officers that Violet had gone crazy with rage when she'd learned that the wilderness guide she'd been having an affair with had been secretly seeing her best friend and maid of honor, Ariel Potter. She'd shot the guide, pushed Ariel over a cliff and then attempted to kill Lance and his best man, Jared Dennis.

According to his story, they had barely managed to escape with their lives. It hadn't taken long to realize the story had been fabricated. Lance had become a suspect in the murder of the wilderness guide, but he and his best man had gone into hiding before they could be taken in for questioning. Since then, Gabe and his fellow troopers had been hunting for the suspects and for Violet. She was the key to understanding what had happened and why.

"I hope he doesn't think she's a tasty little treat," Violet said with a nervous laugh.

"Bear prefers his kibble. He would never take a bite out of a human," he replied, watching as Violet dropped her pack, shrugged out of her coat and took the baby from the sling carrier. "That is one tiny little baby," he commented.

"Ava was born a few weeks early, but the doctor says she's healthy." She settled into a rickety chair that sat against a wall. Despite having recently given birth, she was almost too thin, her face gaunt beneath what looked like a thick layer of makeup. She was a beautiful woman. Nothing could hide or diminish that, but the last seven months had changed her. She wasn't the carefree socialite he'd seen in the photos and newspaper stories. She was somber and scared, her eyes large in her thin face.

"I'm glad to hear that. The wilderness isn't the best place for a newborn baby."

"I know," she agreed. "But I was afraid to return. Lance is dangerous, and I didn't know what he'd do if he got his hands on our baby."

"I understand that, but the two of you will be safer with police protection than out on your own."

She frowned but didn't respond.

After she'd gone missing, Gabe had expected her to succumb to the elements.

She'd survived.

And continued to elude the police.

He admired her gumption, but he wasn't going to risk her escaping again. She needed to answer questions, and he needed to make certain she stayed safe.

"Sounds like she might be hungry," he commented as the baby whimpered.

He didn't know much about infants. Everything he *did* know, he'd learned from hearing coworkers and friends talk about their children. Babies needed to eat, they needed diaper changes and they needed to sleep.

That was the sum of his knowledge.

"She is," Violet responded, pushing to her feet wearily, the baby clutched close to her chest. "I'll go in the back room and feed her."

"No need. I'll go. You stay near the fire."

He grabbed her backpack and parka as he left the room.

He wasn't giving her an opportunity to run off.

"I'm not planning on leaving," she grumbled as he stepped into the larger room. "And the pack has Ava's diapers in it."

He didn't respond. People said a lot of things. Told a lot of lies and a lot of half-truths. Maybe she hadn't planned on leaving. Or maybe she had. But in any event, he wasn't taking chances. Gabe and the K-9 team had been working to close the murder investigation for several months. Violet was the key to doing that. And now that he had her, he didn't plan to let her go.

Plus, whether she wanted to admit it or not, she needed his protection.

As soon as the weather cleared, backup would arrive to transport them out of the park and to the Anchorage police department. He had already contacted the team, sending coordinates so that they could head in as soon as it was safe to do so.

He walked into the back room, checking the window and the door. Neither was secure enough to make him comfortable. If Lance decided to track through the blizzard, if he made it to the cabin, he would try to break in. But, fortunately, that would not be so easy to do without Bear alerting them first.

That was one of the blessings of working with dogs. They had exceptional senses and could hear and smell what humans couldn't.

Gabe pulled out his cell phone. No reception. Not with the storm raging. He knew the team, though. They'd be in as soon as it was possible. He paced the small room, listening to the wind and the groan of old wood. Bear was still in the main room, lying on the floor where he had been told to stay. Probably getting hot with the fire going.

"Bear, free!" he called.

Seconds later, the K-9 padded into the room, his tongue lolling, his tail up, his body relaxed. He sniffed Violet's pack, then sat in front of Gabe.

"Thirsty, buddy?" Gabe guessed, sliding out of his pack and pulling out water and a collapsible bowl. He gave Bear water, then pulled off his coat, hanging it from a peg near the door.

"She's done eating," Violet said quietly, suddenly appearing in the doorway between rooms. "You can come back in here. It's warmer."

"Bear enjoys the cold," he responded.

"Your dog has a thick coat. You don't." She turned before he could respond, the baby's head visible just above her shoulder. Fuzzy white infant curls against the bright blue fabric of Violet's flannel shirt. That wasn't what she had been wearing the last time she was seen by her friend Ariel. Violet's bridesmaid had photos of the day. She'd captured the soon-to-be groom and his best man before they'd left for wedding. Both had looked happy. Violet, dressed in jeans and a cable-knit sweater, had been smiling, but there'd been something in her eyes—a bit of fear or trepidation that had caught Gabe's attention.

She had been pretending to be happy, but she hadn't been.

Regrets?

Misgivings?

Hours later, she'd fled the scene of what should have been her wedding. Gabe and the canine team had found her trail and followed it until the dogs lost the scent.

"Is this where you've been holing up for the past few months?" he asked as he walked back into the main room.

She hesitated, then shook her head. "No."

"A cabin like it?"

"I'd rather not say," she murmured, settling back into the chair.

"Why not?"

"Because… I don't want to betray the trust of people I've come to care about."

"Someone helped you hide?"

She didn't respond.

"I'll take that as an affirmative."

"They didn't do anything wrong, because *I* didn't do anything wrong," she replied. "It isn't like they were harboring a fugitive. They were helping a very scared woman whom they happened to find wandering around in the woods." She shrugged, patting the baby's back as she settled into the chair again.

Violet looked tired, her skin pale through layers of heavy makeup. She'd been hiding for months. Pregnant. Scared. Probably traumatized by what she'd seen and what she'd been through.

She had been betrayed by someone she'd loved. Someone she had planned to marry. That couldn't be an easy thing to deal with.

He'd told himself that he wouldn't have sympathy for her.

She could have turned herself in to the police, gone into protective custody and stayed safe. Instead, she'd stayed a step ahead of the team, always eluding capture and making it difficult for them to do their jobs and finish their investigation.

So, yeah, the hard-nosed cop in him felt that she'd gotten what she'd deserved, and he didn't want his opinion of Violet to soften. But the protector in him? Well, he couldn't help feeling for her. She was young and tired, her sweet, innocent baby sleeping peacefully in her arms. For months, she'd lived in terror, doing everything she could to keep her baby from harm. She had stayed away from everyone and everything she knew to keep her child from harm.

He could respect that.

He could understand it.

In her position, he'd probably have done the same.

"We could have helped you," he said sternly. "If you'd turned yourself in to the authorities, we'd have kept you safe."

"How? By locking me in a jail cell? I heard news reports, and I know you thought of me as the prime suspect in the crime."

"For a short period of time, we did. But it didn't take us long to sort things out."

"You thought I was culpable," she pointed out. "I heard the reports. The police were calling me a person of interest."

"We still are," he said. "We have questions that need answering. Ariel didn't see who pushed her off the cliff, and she has no idea who killed the wilderness guide you hired."

"How is Ariel?" she interrupted, leaning forward, her eyes deeply shadowed. "I've been worried sick about her."

"She's made a full recovery, but she's spent seven months worrying about you."

"I know," she said quietly, her gaze shifting away. She had to have thought it all through, weighed all her options, all the people she would worry, all the responsibilities she was abandoning. Somehow, in her mind, staying hidden had been the only viable option.

He couldn't understand the decision, but he couldn't help respecting it.

"But you still stayed away. Why? What happened that made you think that was your only option?" he asked, curious to hear her version of what had happened all those months ago.

"I saw Jared Dennis push her off a cliff. I'd run to get her after…"

"What?"

She swallowed hard, the memory obviously upsetting. "I found Cal. He was bleeding. I felt for a pulse but couldn't find one. I ran for Ariel's help, and I saw Jared shove her off the cliff. She was taking pictures of eagles. Minding her own business. She tried to save herself, but she toppled over. I screamed, and Jared came after me. He was yelling for Lance to grab the gun and take care of me. I didn't even know they'd brought a gun on the trip. I had to run, but all I could think about was my friend tumbling over the cliff and Cal lying on the ground." Her voice broke.

"You did what you had to," he assured her, knowing she had to be carrying a terrible burden of guilt.

"There might have been something else I could have done. I don't know. It all happened so fast, and it was all so confusing. If I had just been thinking about myself, I might have gone back toward our vehicles, but that seemed like the obvious choice, and I was worried Lance would catch me before I could escape. I had learned I was pregnant two weeks before, and I knew I wasn't just running to save my life. There was another life to worry about."

"You can't beat yourself up over what happened. You did what you had to. You know that, right?"

"Sometimes," she responded. "Other times, I think that if I had made better choices, Cal would still be alive and Ariel wouldn't have been injured."

"Better choices?"

"I…wasn't always certain of how much Lance loved me. I wanted to believe the things he said, but his actions didn't always bear up to the emotions he claimed to feel."

"Meaning?"

"I think he wanted my money more than he wanted me." She said it dispassionately, but he could see the pain in her eyes.

"What does that have to do with Cal's murder and Ariel being pushed off the cliff?" he asked, curious to know what she thought her former fiancé's motive had been.

She shrugged. "I don't know, but I'm sure Lance had something to do with both things. Jared is a follower. He does what he's told."

That had been Gabe's impression as well. During questioning, Jared had given what sounded like scripted responses that perfectly matched the information Lance provided. No veering from the topic. No adding extra details. That had been Gabe's first indication that both men were being deceptive.

"What happened after you ran?" he asked, switching gears before she got upset enough to shut down.

"I tossed my phone over the side of a hill. Lance had a tracking app, and I was afraid he'd be able to find me. I was trying to get on the trail so I could return to the vehicles and get help, but I got turned around and ended up wandering deeper into the park."

"You spent that night in the woods?" He and the team had scoured the area, but Chugach State Park was vast. The dogs had found and lost her scent numerous times before sunset. They'd suspended the search until dawn and began again the next day.

"Yes. I tried to find my way out the next morning, but I was so turned around, I had no idea which way to walk. That's when I ran into…" She shook her head. "I was found by some survivalists. They took me in."

That made sense.

He and the team had been certain she would succumb to the elements. She'd had no survivalist training and hadn't been prepared to stay outside for any length of time.

"And helped you for the past seven months."

"Yes." The answer was terse, her gaze dropping. She was uncomfortable with the direction of the conversation. Either she was lying, or she was worried about getting the people who'd helped her in trouble.

"We aren't going to charge them with anything, Violet," he said. "But we'll probably want to talk to them. A name and location would be helpful."

"I'm not providing either."

No apology. Or explanation. She was still looking away, her gaze focused on the fire, her hand resting on the baby's back. Snow had melted in her hair and dripped down her temple, leaving white tracks through her heavy makeup. She was exhausted, scared and still willing to stand up for what she believed in, still intent on protecting people who had protected her.

He respected and admired that. He'd thought she would be spoiled, haughty and demanding.

She wasn't any of those things.

Realizing that made him want to be gentle rather than tough. Good cop rather than bad cop. He was known for his tough-as-nails approach to the job, but he couldn't be tough with someone who had been through so much and fought so hard to protect others.

"Why not?" he asked.

"Because they helped me when I needed it most, and they don't want to be found. If I bring civilization to them, how is that repayment for all they've done?"

"I understand your feelings, but we need to ask what they saw the day of the murder, what they heard, if they have anything to add to our investigation."

"Like I said, I'm not giving you that information." She pressed her lips together, her muscles tense.

"That's fine. For now. We'll discuss it again once we get out of here," he responded gruffly, his heart softer toward her than he wanted it to be. He wouldn't take no for an answer. He *couldn't*. They'd been chasing down leads for months, trying to find Violet so that they could get her version of events. They had wanted to question her about Lance, their relationship, his habits. He and his buddy Jared had taken off as soon as they'd realized the focus of the investigation had shifted to them.

They'd been on the run ever since.

Why they hadn't left the area was a mystery that needed to be solved. Most criminals fled and went into hiding far from the scene of their crimes.

Lance and Jared had stayed local, eluding police by using the park and the vast wilderness that surrounded Anchorage. They weren't survivalists. They were scavengers and predators, breaking into winterized cabins, using them for shelter until unwary owners showed up.

Bear lifted his head, his gaze focused on the window. He growled, his attention never wavering as he charged toward the glass and barked.

"What's wrong?" Violet asked, pulling the baby close as she stood and moved to the back of the room. Away from the window and whatever or whoever was outside.

"Could be an animal," he responded, but Bear wasn't the kind of dog to bark at wildlife.

"You don't really think that, do you?" She looked scared, her muscles tense, her gaze riveted to the door as if she expected someone to kick it open.

"I'll check it out," Gabe told her. He wasn't going to lie about the potential danger, but he didn't want to scare her more than she already was. And he certainly didn't want her running into the blizzard with her newborn. She'd survived the first time she'd fled in terror. She might not be as fortunate the second time around.

He closed ratty fabric curtains over the windows, blocking some of the grayish light that had filtered through the glass. Then grabbed his coat and pack, quickly sliding into both.

"Stay away from the windows, and don't open the door until I tell you to."

"I—I won't. Be careful. Too many people have already been hurt because of me. I don't want you to be another tragedy."

"Don't worry. I know how to take care of myself," he assured her, smiling to try to reassure her that everything was going to be okay.

Then he pulled the door open and stepped into the storm. Bear barreled out beside him, nose up to the wind, fur ruffled by it. The dog's thick coat would keep him warm for a while.

"What do you think, Bear? Anyone out here?" He surveyed the small clearing in front of the cabin. His K-9 partner was a few feet away, staying close until he was told to search. Until Gabriel knew what they were hunting, he wouldn't send the St. Bernard out. Bear was a large target, strong and powerful but not trained to attack. He would defend himself if necessary, but he wasn't going to take down an armed criminal the way other dogs on the team might.

Bear veered right, heading toward the edge of the woods. Gabriel pushed a branch aside as he walked into the forest, his ears straining for any unusual sounds. It was impossible to hear more than the howling of the wind and the groaning of trees bending beneath its fury. Gabe had GPS coordinates for the cabin and wasn't concerned about finding it again. His top priority was tracking down Lance. Seven months into the murder investigation, and he and the team were ready to get the perps into custody. As long as Lance and Jared were on the streets, no one in Alaska was safe.

He edged deeper into the woods, watching as Bear sniffed the ground, then dropped down to his haunches. He'd found something. A boot print pressed into snow and dirt, leading away from the cabin.

Had a transient walked through? Maybe thinking about using the cabin during the storm and then realizing it was occupied? It was possible.

It was also possible that Lance had found them and had run when he'd heard the dog bark.

"Let's go," he said, still not willing to give Bear the command to find. Lance was dangerous. If he was out there, he wouldn't hesitate to kill anyone or anything that tried to prevent his escape.

Bear growled and swung his head to the left, his body suddenly stiff, his muscles taut.

Gabriel stepped behind a tree.

A bullet slammed into the rugged pine, splinters of bark and wood hitting his face. He dived to the ground, blood oozing from a gash in his temple as he pulled his weapon and fired.

THREE

Violet could hear nothing over the wild roar of the wind. The old cabin shook beneath the onslaught, the windows rattling with the fury of the storm.

She needed to feed the fire.

She needed to change Ava.

She needed to plan what she would do if Gabriel Runyon didn't return.

Violet had almost begged him not to go out into the storm. She had too many horrible memories of the day she'd fled into the wilderness. Back then, she'd felt helpless and alone, the faith that she'd turned her back on after her parents died suddenly the only thing that stood between her and abject hopelessness.

God is present always.

Waiting for us to turn to Him.

Her parents had instilled that in her—the idea that God cared and that He would intervene in the lives of His people. But as she had entered her teenage years, she'd fallen away from their teachings. She'd begun to question their faith, and she'd wondered if God really was concerned about the matters of men.

Didn't He have more important things to do? More vital matters to worry about? Her life had been easy and good. She'd had parents who had loved her. Everything she'd needed and most of the things she'd wanted. She'd had no reason to need God's help.

Violet had stopped attending church in her early twenties.

She regretted that now. Regretted that her parents had died worried about her faith and eternal security. Regretted that they hadn't lived long enough to know that she finally understood how deeply she needed God in her life.

"You can't live in regrets, Violet," she muttered. "You've got to live in the moment. Do what has to be done right now. Prepare for what will need to be done later."

Those were things she had learned from the Seavers.

They hadn't survived years in the Alaskan wilderness by sitting idly. Rather, they spent their days pursuing the things that would help them survive and thrive. During the spring and summer, they planted, hunted and foraged. In the fall, they harvested and preserved fruits, vegetables and meats. And in the winter, they hunkered down, tending to daily chores while the weather raged.

Violet didn't want to spend her life in their underground bunker, but she had become stronger, more confident and more capable because of her time there.

She sure wasn't the same idealistic young bride-to-be who had ventured into the wilderness seven months ago—a rich, spoiled socialite playing at understanding the great outdoors. She had become someone who could light a fire, build a shelter, raise a baby without help. She was independent, strong, and filled with a desire to raise her daughter to be the same.

She didn't need or want anyone in her life.

All she wanted was to be able to return home. She wanted to give Ava a warm house with windows that let in the light, a backyard with views of the mountains and the security that came from a roof overhead and neighbors nearby. She understood that the Seavers didn't need or want those things, but Violet craved them. More with each passing day.

"Focus," she grumbled, grabbing a few logs from the stack and tepeeing them over the flames.

"Always tend your fire first, Ava," she said. "Shelter and warmth are your first priority when you're out in the wilderness."

Ava stirred, her soft hair brushing against Violet's jaw as she burrowed closer. She was too tiny to understand the lessons Violet wanted to teach, but eventually she would be old enough to learn.

"Right, precious girl?" she murmured against the baby's hair, her heart thudding painfully as the windows and doors rattled. She was trying to focus on the job at hand, but her mind was skipping from thought to thought.

Was Lance outside?

What would he do if he found her?

Kill her for sure, but what about the baby? *His* baby? Would he murder his own flesh and blood?

Or would he take Ava to some far-off place and raise her?

Either thought was horrifying.

"But we're not going to think about that. We're going to concentrate on keeping the fire going and staying one step ahead of trouble."

She grabbed her coat and shrugged into it, then opened the back door, scooping snow into an old pot that had been left on a shelf near the fireplace.

If they got snowed in, they'd need water. Plenty of it.

Violet tried not to think about Gabriel and his dog out in the storm, possibly being stalked by a predator. She certainly didn't want to imagine Lance outside the cabin, watching as she set the pot on the fire, so she focused on the task at hand, then quickly changed Ava.

Suddenly, something bumped the back door.

She jumped, spinning to face it.

As if, somehow, watching danger's arrival could make it less horrible.

"Please, God, don't let it be Lance. You've protected us for this long. Please keep us safe awhile longer," she prayed aloud, her lips pressed to Ava's downy curls.

The door shook as something slammed into it again.

She stepped back, using her free arm to blindly search for a weapon. There was an ancient rifle standing in the corner behind the rocking chair. Not loaded. No ammunition. Months ago, she and Harrison Seaver had stopped in the cabin on the way back from the clinic. The place had been abandoned long ago, the old rifle left to gather dust and rust. It probably wasn't functional, but it might scare someone away.

She placed Ava back in the carrier, relieved when she snuggled in easily. Then she checked the rifle's cartridge chamber. Empty. Just as she had expected.

She could use the heavy wooden weapon as a club or

as a scare tactic. No one who hadn't been in the cabin would know it wasn't loaded.

There hadn't been another thud or bang. The wind was still howling, cold seeping through her layers, her body shaking.

She was cold.

She was scared.

She was alone.

Just as she had been when she had run into the wilderness to escape Lance and Jared.

She hadn't known the area. Hadn't known how to survive the late-spring temperatures, which fell to below freezing at night. But she'd had no choice. Jared and Lance had been chasing her, Lance screaming that she was going to be sorry if she didn't stop running. She hadn't stopped.

She had run until she was out of breath, her heart skipping beats, her legs trembling. Then she had found a hole left by the roots of a fallen tree. She had crawled in and stayed there.

After the sun had set, and she was certain she had escaped, she had climbed hills attempting to see the lights of Anchorage. All she had discerned was darkness. By the time the Seavers had found her, she was dehydrated, hungry and wanted by the police.

She was a different person now…and she needed to remember that.

Something slammed into the front door again, and she ran in that direction, rifle in hand, pointed at the shuddering wood.

"I have a gun!" she announced, waiting for the old wood to be kicked in and for Lance to appear.

A dog barked, the sound carrying over the wild howl of the wind.

"Bear?" She yanked open the door, slamming it shut after the giant dog barreled in.

Snow-covered, tongue lolling.

Alone.

"Where's Gabriel?" she asked, as if the dog could respond.

He whirled back to the door, scratching the wood frantically.

"Is he hurt?"

Worse?

She opened the door again, hoping the ruggedly handsome trooper would be there. But she couldn't see anything. Visibility was almost zero, the snow swirling in a thick cloud of white.

Bear grabbed the hem of her shirt, tugging her outside.

"No," she yelped, pulling back.

Undeterred, the dog moved behind her, nudged her toward the door, whining loudly. Melting snow dripped from his coat and muzzle, his dark eyes focused on Violet, asking her for something.

"All right. I get it. You need me to help you find Gabriel," she said as she pulled rope from her emergency pack and tied it to her waist, her heart pounding crazily in her chest. Something horrible must have happened for Bear to have returned without Gabriel. She didn't want to imagine what that could be. She only knew she had to try to find and help him.

She'd go as far as the length of the rope. No farther. It would be too difficult to find her way back in this storm if she weren't tethered to the cabin. And she couldn't subject her baby to these harsh elements for long. She walked outside and tied the other end of the rope to a tree near the front door, fighting the wind, struggling to see Bear through the whiteout conditions.

Please, God, she prayed silently as snow pelted her face and the wind stole her breath, *help me find him.*

Bear stayed close as she struggled forward, seemingly unfazed by the blustering storm.

"Okay. Slow and steady," she muttered, giving the rope a hard tug to make certain it wouldn't untie. She had the rifle under her arm, Ava close to her chest, her hood pulled up over her hair. She was already cold. Already wondering if she was making the right decision. She had to protect her daughter.

But she couldn't leave Gabriel out in the storm.

Bear barked, his big body so close, her free hand brushed against his shoulder. She hooked her fingers through a strap on his vest, determined to stay tethered to him as they walked farther from safety and deeper into the storm.

Snow swirled in thick waves of white, limiting visibility to just a few feet. No lights in sight. No sign of the cabin. Any footprints he and Bear had left were covered by fresh snowfall. It couldn't be much farther to the cabin. Gabe counted paces out. He knew how much distance he had traveled—he had marked the cabin location on his GPS and had been following that back—but satellite reception was iffy in this kind of weather.

Still, he knew they had to be close.

The fact that Bear had charged ahead seemed to confirm it, but five feet was too much when a person was hypothermic.

Which he was.

His feet and hands were numb, his body shaking with cold. He had been outside too long. Even dressed right, a person could only last so long outside in weather like this. Soon his body would stop trying to produce heat. Blood would be shuttled to his vital organs. Everything else would shut down. His brain functions would slow, and he'd start making poor decisions.

He knew all the facts. He had studied them in emergency preparation classes, wilderness first aid and search management courses.

He needed to get to shelter before he became a statistic.

Gabe glanced at the GPS unit. A moving light tracked Bear's movements. He was two hundred meters straight ahead. Moving slowly in Bear's direction, trying desperately to close the distance between them. He wanted to rush, but he needed to be careful. Deadfall was slippery on good days. During inclement weather, the old logs and branches were hidden hazards that could easily cause broken bones.

He couldn't afford to be injured.

"You can't afford to be hypothermic, either," he muttered, wishing the storm wasn't preventing the K-9 unit's arrival. Gabe had sent coordinates as soon as he had located Violet. He trusted the men and women he worked with and knew they would be there as quickly as they could, but traveling in whiteout conditions wasn't possible.

That meant he would have to deal with Lance on his own.

And if Lance had his buddy Jared with him, and the men were still out in the storm, Gabriel would have to face down both.

He'd been certain he'd heard an ATV motor just after he'd fired a warning shot into the storm. Based on Bear's more relaxed behavior, he'd felt confident the shooter had backed off.

For now.

He touched his forehead. The blood had stopped oozing from the wound. He stumbled through ankle-deep snow, his focus on the yellow blip on his GPS screen. He was closing in on it. Once he reached Bear, he knew he could get back to the cabin. The St. Bernard had an uncanny ability to find his way through snow. He could find a missing person in some of the most challenging terrain. There was no way he wasn't going to be able to get them back to Violet.

Gabriel stopped, listening for the unmistakable sound of Bear's excited barks. He heard nothing. Usually his K-9 partner would be running toward him, eager to be reunited. Gabe had no doubt that Bear could smell him. The wind was moving toward the dog, sending a scent cone that even a rookie search dog would be able to follow.

So why wasn't he running? Or barking?

Gabe waited impatiently while the wind howled and snow flew in his face. When the blip was nearly on top of him, he could finally see the outline of Bear. Someone was with him. Dark against the white landscape, holding him by the collar. Not tall like Lance or Jared.

Violet?

Had she left the safety of the cabin?

That hadn't occurred to him, but it probably should have. She'd been on her own for months, learning to survive in the wilderness, sometimes sneaking in and out of Anchorage without being seen.

The ornery woman certainly wouldn't hesitate to run if she thought it was necessary, but he doubted that she was trying to escape in the storm. She'd come looking for him.

Bear barked. Just once.

"Good boy," Gabriel called. "Stay."

The dog stopped, and Violet followed suit.

Then they both stood and waited as Gabriel approached, Bear shifting excitedly, Violet looking tense and unsure.

"Gabriel?" she called as he drew closer.

"If it wasn't, Bear would be letting you know," he responded, sliding his arm around her slender waist and turning her toward the cabin. He could feel smooth rope beneath his finger. She'd taken precautions.

That was good. What would be better was getting them both back inside the cabin. "Are you okay? I was worried when Bear came back without you," she shouted above the howling wind.

"I'll be better once we're both inside," he admitted. "Bear, lead!" he commanded.

The St. Bernard took off, loping in front of them, a dark shadow against the snow.

Gabe kept him in sight, fighting the urge to rush. Violet had the baby strapped to her chest, tucked away under a coat. They were both vulnerable, both in need of protection. Until the team was able to get through the storm, he and Bear were all they had.

It would be a long night. Even longer if Lance decided to reappear. Gabriel hoped that wouldn't happen, but if it did, he was prepared to do whatever it took to keep Violet and her baby safe.

FOUR

Violet wanted to run back to the cabin, but she was afraid of falling and injuring Ava. She moved cautiously, using the rope as a guide. Thankfully, she could see Bear, walking in front, leading the way. But he was a dog, and she was worried he'd take off after a moose or decide to chase a scent in the wind.

The last thing she needed was more time outside in the storm. She was already shivering. So was Gabriel. She could feel him shaking violently as they made their way through the storm.

"We're almost there," she said, hoping she was right.

It felt like they'd been walking forever, pushing against the wind and hiking through the snow.

"There it is," Gabriel said.

"Where?" Violet couldn't see anything but white. Snow. Trees. Wind. All of it a misty blanket that shrouded the world. Beside her, Gabe was a solid and comforting presence, his arm around her waist, his fingers pressing against her ribs.

She didn't want to need anyone.

Not after what she had been through.

But she pressed closer to Gabe's side, relieved that she wasn't in this alone. That she had someone standing beside her, fighting the battle with her. They would survive together.

Or die together.

She refused the thought.

She was a fighter.

She would fight through this, and she would come out the other side better and stronger and more capable.

"Straight ahead. I caught a glimpse when the wind shifted." Gabe's hand tightened on her waist, and his fingers pressed against her ribs. He oozed confidence and self-assurance, towering over her in a way that was protective rather than intimidating.

"Are you sure?" she asked, shivering from the cold, terrified for her daughter.

"Absolutely," he responded. "It's just a little farther."

"I hope you're right," she replied, her words swallowed by the storm. She had no choice but to trust him, to move with him as he took one step after another. She had just met him, but she was putting her life and the life of her child in his hands.

That was a strange and uncomfortable feeling, but she would rather be in this with someone than alone.

A few more steps, and she could see the dark wall of the cabin.

Bear was waiting by the door. If he was cold, he didn't show it.

Gabriel dragged the door open, holding it against the wind as Violet stepped inside. The fire was still going, the snow melted and boiling. She hurried to it, using a fireplace poker to move the pot from the flames.

"That's quite a storm," Gabriel said, closing the door and dropping the heavy latch into place.

"Hopefully it'll keep Lance away," she responded, taking off her coat and hanging it over the back of a chair. Ava still seemed content, sleeping soundly in her sling. Hair dry. Skin warm. She had weathered the journey well.

Meanwhile, Violet felt frozen to the bone.

She crouched near the flames, taking off her gloves and holding her hands out to the warmth. "I boiled water. How about some tea?" she suggested as Gabriel joined her.

"I've got soup. How about that instead?" he suggested, shrugging out of his pack and pulling out several packets of freeze-dried food. "Chicken noodle or tomato?"

"Chicken noodle," she replied.

She wouldn't say no to calories. She'd lost too much weight after Ava's birth, and she couldn't afford to go into the winter any thinner than she already was. The Seavers ate sparely during the coldest months, and she was nursing a baby. She had to stay healthy enough to continue nourishing her daughter.

But eating had lost its appeal after Ava's birth.

She'd felt melancholy and tired, unmotivated and ambivalent. The thought of spending winter in the underground bunker filled her with dread. She wanted to go home. She wanted Ava to have her own bed rather than sharing with Violet.

A crib would be nice. As would a rocking chair and changing table... "You okay?" Gabriel asked.

He was holding out a steaming bowl of rehydrated soup.

She took it, her hands still nearly frozen, her fingers curving around the warm porcelain. "I'm fine."

"You don't look fine." He opened a packet of soup, dumped it into the other bowl and ladled water out of the pot with a mug he'd taken from his pack.

"That's just what every woman wants to hear."

"I'm not here to make you feel good. I'm here to make sure you stay safe," he muttered, sipping the soup and watching her over the rim of the bowl.

"I was plenty safe until this morning. I'm not sure how Lance found me, but I'm not going to give him another opportunity. Once I get back to the bunker…"

She realized she was saying too much, staring into his eyes and forgetting that he was a police officer. For all she knew, he might come down hard on the family that had harbored her when she'd been wanted by the police.

"The bunker?" he asked, setting his soup on the hearth and taking a collapsible bowl from his pack. He used his water bladder to fill it, setting it down in front of Bear, who lapped greedily.

"I told you. I was helped by a family. That's where they live. In the bunker."

"In a national park?" He raised a dark eyebrow.

"And this is why I refused to give you information about them," she responded, taking a careful sip of the soup.

"Hey, I have no authority in the park, and I'm not questioning you so that I can go in and disturb a family that isn't bothering anyone," he replied. "I'm just curious."

"Why?"

"Because that's what I do. I get curious, I ask questions, I get answers. It's part of the job." He shrugged. "So, you've been living in a bunker. That explains why drones and airplanes couldn't spot you."

"It isn't like I had a choice," she replied.

Violet hadn't meant to cause trouble. She certainly hadn't wanted the police to send out drones and planes to find her. All along she'd been doing what she thought was right. And had been prepared to go to any lengths to protect her baby. She still was, but she thought she might be able to trust Gabe to help her, to get her to civilization and help her navigate the legal ramifications of the choices she had made. "I understand you felt that way," he said gently, his eyes the deep blue of the sky at dusk.

How many evenings had she spent sitting outside the bunker, staring up at sky? Watching as the moon rose and the stars appeared? How many times had she wished she wasn't so alone? Even with the Seavers nearby, she had felt isolated. She had longed to have someone to sit beside late at night when she couldn't sleep, when worries and fears kept her awake.

She'd turned to her faith for comfort, reaching out to God in those horrible dark days after Cal's murder, but she had still wanted human companionship and friendship. The Seavers had been wonderful, but they saw the world in a vastly different way.

"I didn't just *feel* that way. I ran from Lance thinking I could go to the police and get the protection I needed. By the next day, it was all over the news that I was the primary suspect in two assaults and a homicide. I couldn't just turn myself in and hope for the best.

Not when I had a baby to think about." Violet got to her feet, carrying the soup across the room and settling into the chair. She was still cold, but she didn't want to sit close to Gabriel. She didn't want him looking into her eyes and seeing the shame and guilt there.

If she wasn't terrified for her life, and that of her un-born child, she would have had the Seavers bring her to the police station, and she would have turned herself it.

"I understand," he said, still watching her.

She expected more questions.

Thought he'd be filled with recriminations.

After all, she'd spent seven months eluding police. But instead, he remained silent. She tried to wait out the quiet the way she had done so many times when she lived with the Seavers. Dana was warm and caring, but she was a woman of few words, and Violet had learned to wait and give her a chance to speak.

But Gabriel didn't seem compelled to fill the silence.

In many ways, he was an enigma, and a part of her wanted to find out what made him tick. He hadn't hunted her down and interrogated her harshly. She would have understood if he had. She'd been hiding from the police, eluding capture, for months, and he had to have been frustrated by that.

But he had been gentle, kind and compassionate. He hadn't pushed hard for the things he obviously wanted. He'd asked questions and let her answer, giving her space to think things through.

She studied his profile as he sat in front of the fire, sipping hot soup, a bloody scratch on his temple. He was handsome. There was no denying that. Masculine and strong, with a soft side that he might not allow everyone to see.

"You're hurt," she said, nervous energy forcing the words out. She shouldn't be noticing the way he looked, or the warmth that filled her when he met her eyes.

"My head?" He touched the scratch. "It's fine."

"What happened?"

He hesitated. "Someone took a shot at me. He missed, but I got hit by shrapnel."

"Lance shot at you?" She wasn't shocked. She was appalled. The thought that someone she'd loved could do something so horrible filled her with guilt and remorse.

"Probably, it was Lance, but I don't know that for sure," he told her.

"Who else would shoot at a police officer?"

"Plenty of people, actually. I've made some enemies during my time on the force," he said with a tired smile.

"I'm sorry," she replied softly. "I wish that weren't the case."

"If wishes were horses, beggars would ride," he replied, unzipping his coat and finally removing it.

He had been outside longer than Violet, and he was still shivering from it. He had done so much to help her, and she'd let him sit there shivering and cold while she warmed up near the fire.

"There are blankets in the trunk," she said, pointing to the old cot and the trunk that sat beside it. "I can get one for you. You've been out in the cold awhile, and you need to warm up."

"I'll get them. With the way the wind is blowing through this place, it's going to be difficult to stay warm. Even with a fire." He walked to the trunk and pulled out several wool blankets. He draped one around his shoulders and put another around hers, tugging the ends so that they covered Ava. "Hopefully, the baby won't be too cold tonight."

"She should be fine," she managed, secretly touched by the overture. "The Seavers…"

She pressed her lips together, frustrated that she'd said the name. She had no intention of giving any information about them to the police. They'd helped her more than anyone else could have, and she owed them her life.

"*Seavers?*" he asked, settling down near the fire again.

Bear had made himself comfortable, spreading out near the front door, his quiet snores indicating that all was right in his world.

"Forget I said that," she replied, finishing her soup and setting the bowl on the floor beside the chair. She was too tired to stand. Caring for an infant was hard work. Caring for one out in the wilderness was even harder. There were no electric lights. No quick way to warm up water. No tub. No real shower. The Seavers relied on candles for light and propane for heat. Washing clothes required muscle power and time.

Her hands were raw from scrubbing diapers and onesies.

Dana seemed to love the lifestyle. But Violet? Well, she wasn't quite as enamored.

Not that she was unappreciative. On the contrary, she was truly grateful for all the Seavers had done for her and Ava. But deep down she longed for normalcy. She craved the hustle and bustle of civilization, the hum of a heater and the purr of motors. The sounds of voices carrying through the evening air.

"I wish I could forget what you said, but unfortunately, I can't," he replied. "There's a guy that I work with who has been searching for Cole Seaver. Any relation to the people you've been staying with?"

Violet hesitated.

She knew what this was about and couldn't in good conscience pretend otherwise. Harrison had recently filled her in about his encounter with Trooper Poppy Walsh, who had told him that she was searching for the Seavers because of a dying woman's last wish to be reunited with her son and his family.

"Yes," she finally admitted.

"It's important that we speak to him. His mother is terminal."

"He knows."

Gabriel frowned. "He does?"

"Harrison ran into a state trooper who shared the information."

"Harrison?"

"Cole's teenage son," she explained. "We've been trying to talk Cole into returning to town to visit his mother, but it's a hard sell."

"Why?"

"I don't really know. He won't say what happened, but whatever it was, he's still angry about it."

"Anger isn't a good reason to deny a mother's dying wish," Gabriel said harshly.

"I agree. If my parents were still around, I wouldn't let anything stand in the way of my being with them. I told Cole that, but he said I didn't understand the dynamics." She had never seen Cole angry like that before. In fact, in all the months she'd lived with the Seavers, he had never raised his voice. He was kind, faith-filled, reasonable and loving, but when it came to his relationship with his mother, he refused to budge.

"I hope he changes his mind," Gabe said, pulling out his phone and frowning. "Looks like my colleagues are trying to get out to us. I'm going to see if I can get through to them on the phone."

He stood, dropping the blanket onto her legs as he walked past and taking a moment to make certain it was wrapped around her thighs. She shivered involuntarily. It was still warm from his body, the heavy wool giving an extra layer of protection from the cold seeping through log walls.

"Thank you," she whispered, but he had already stepped into the back room.

To Gabriel's surprise, the call went through, Hunter McCord picking up on the first ring.

"Gabriel?" he asked, his voice tinged with worry. "Do you have shelter? The weather is horrible, and it isn't going to let up until the early-morning hours."

"Yes. In an old cabin. We've got a fire going and enough wood to keep us warm until the storm breaks. Any idea when the team will be able to deploy?" The sooner the better. He felt safe enough for now, but as soon as the storm let up, Lance would be on the move again. If he didn't already know where the cabin was, the smoke coming out of the chimney would give away their location.

"Should be around dawn," Hunter replied. "We're

hoping to be out before first light. We've already gathered the team, and we'll deploy as soon as we can get all-terrain vehicles out. Any sign of Lance or Jared?"

"Someone shot at me. I'm fairly certain it was one of them, but I think they've left the area. No way are they waiting outside in this mess." He paced to the window, pulled back the tattered curtains and watched the snow swirl. There was no sign of anyone or anything. The fact was, Lance would be a fool to be out on a night like this one. He might be a criminal, but he was a smart one.

"I don't like that he knows where you are. If he's found a place close by to wait out the storm, he could be on you before we arrive."

"I'm prepared," Gabriel assured him.

"I have no doubt about that, but it's not just you I'm worried about. What about Violet James? Is she cooperating?"

"Cooperating?"

"Not trying to run again? Not causing any kind of trouble? With Lance and his buddy out there, you have enough to worry about without having to chase her down in a storm."

"She's…quiet." Gabe glanced at the doorway to the main room. He doubted Violet could hear above the storm, but he lowered his voice. "And cautious. I don't think she trusts that I have her best interest at heart."

"I can't say I blame her. She's been hiding for months. Terrified for months. She probably has no idea who she can count on."

"She also has a baby to protect."

"So, the reports that she was at the clinic with a newborn were accurate." It wasn't a question, but Gabe responded.

"Yes. I don't know much about kids, but this one is tiny. Violet is definitely concerned about protecting her. If nothing else motivates her, that should keep her from attempting an escape."

"There's that, then. How does she seem? I'm sure Ariel will ask."

"The baby? Fine. Violet? Tired. Too thin. Stressed," he responded. "It might not be a bad idea to get Ariel involved. She could assure Violet that we only have her best interest at heart."

"If you're suggesting a phone conversation, I'm all for it."

"I was thinking more along the lines of a meeting when we get back to Anchorage." A phone conversation would be fine, but he thought that the best thing for Violet would be to see her friend face-to-face. Familiarity and comfort could go a long way in helping her open up about what she'd seen and experienced.

"That's not happening until we've apprehended Lance and Jared," Hunter growled. "I don't want to give that guy any reason to think he should go after Ariel again. She's safe as long as she stays away from Violet."

Gabe could have argued that the team could keep Ariel safe, but he understood Hunter's concerns for the woman he loved. She had nearly been killed. He didn't want to risk putting her in harm's way. No matter how small the chance that she'd be hurt. "Understood. The good news is that Violet's version of events substantiates our belief that she is innocent of the crimes she was being accused of. When I questioned her about what happened in Chugach State Park that day, she told me she found the guide dead, ran to get help and saw Ariel pushed off the cliff. She thought for sure she was dead, so she took off, hoping to get help. And it was only later on that she learned her best friend had survived."

"Yeah, that matches with the evidence and with what little Ariel can remember about that day." Hunter always sounded soft when he spoke of Ariel Potter. She'd survived a lot, and she'd proven to be tough and resilient. It hadn't surprised anyone on the team when the two had fallen in love.

"From what I've been able to gather, Violet stayed hidden because she was afraid of Lance. She was afraid going to the police would make her an easier target," Gabe continued.

"She has good reason to be. Did she give you any idea as to why he wouldn't just flee the area?"

"The conversations haven't gotten that far," he said. "She's guarded, and I don't want to push. She seems… fragile."

"She's been surviving in the wilderness alone, Gabe. *Fragile* isn't a word I'd use to describe her."

"She hasn't been alone. She was taken in by a survivalist family. Get this," he said, glancing at the doorway again. "She's been staying with Cole Seaver and his wife and son."

"Cole Seaver, the guy Eli has been searching for?"

"Yes."

"Strange coincidence."

"I don't put much stock in coincidence. I'd call it an act of divine intervention. Violet has been trying to convince Cole to see his mother before she dies."

"I'll pass that information along to Eli," Hunter promised. "He'll be happy to hear that someone is trying to help."

The team's tech guru, Eli Partridge, was close to his dying godmother—Cole Seaver's mother—and he was determined to make her last wish come true.

"I appreciate it."

"And I'll appreciate it if you stay in one piece until the team can get to you in the morning," Hunter deadpanned.

"I'll keep that in mind," he said. "Text when you're heading my way."

"Will do." Hunter ended the call, and Gabriel shoved the phone in his pocket. Hopefully he could check in with the team during the night, but the storm wasn't abating, so the chances were low.

He was on his own until morning.

Well, not quite alone.

He had Bear. The dog might be a lover rather than a fighter, but he was a great early-warning system. If anyone approached, he would let Gabriel know.

In the meantime, he was going to make good use of the time he had with Violet. There was more to her story, and he had every intention of hearing it. He needed all the details, every bit of information that she could offer.

Once he got her to safety, he planned to go after Lance, and Violet might be the key to understanding how her former fiancé thought and how he might act.

Information was the key to successfully stopping a cold-blooded killer, and Gabriel wasn't opposed to twisting arms to get what he needed.

But something about Violet made him hesitate to use a more aggressive approach.

He might be a hard-nosed, hard-hitting cop, but he had a soft spot for the underdogs.

In this situation, Violet was that.

She had everything against her. No background in survival, no experience in the wilderness, absolutely no skills that would have helped her survive.

Somehow, she had done it.

He respected that and her.

He might need answers, but he was going to be gentle in his approach to getting them. She deserved that and more, after everything she'd been through.

FIVE

No crib.

No bed.

One musty cot sitting against a log wall.

Despite the fire, the cabin was cold. Not a good place to settle a newborn down for the night. But that was fine. Violet had experienced plenty of sleepless nights during her wilderness exile. When she'd first been taken in by the Seavers, she'd lain awake staring into the darkness, terrified that Lance would find her. After Ava's birth, she'd worried that something would happen to the baby. She'd wondered if the dirt walls of the bunker were safe for little lungs, and she'd been afraid that Ava would fall asleep and not wake.

Staying awake all night was easy. But spending the night in a cabin with a stranger was far more complicated. Because she didn't trust people...not anymore. Gabriel might wear a badge and carry a gun, he might be kind and protective, but she didn't plan to put any faith in him.

Sighing, she watched as he walked to the trunk and emptied it. There were several old quilts and a few threadbare flannel shirts. No mice or other critters. She was thankful for that. She had gotten used to sharing space with shelter-seeking animals, but she still didn't like it.

"This might work for the baby," he said, carrying the crate across the room and setting it closer to the fire.

"I don't mind holding her." She loved being a mother. After all the horrible things that had happened since she'd met Lance, having a baby in her arms felt a little like redemption, renewal and hope.

"You need rest. You're a new mother, and you've been through a lot these past few months." He dragged the cot next to the trunk, folded two flannel shirts and used them to pad the trunk. "If you don't want to lay her in here, I can hold her while you sleep."

She lifted a brow. "Do you have any experience with babies?"

"No, but I raised a puppy who got into a lot more trouble than your baby seems capable of. And he survived." He smiled, obviously trying to lighten the mood. Maybe trying to create camaraderie and work on gaining her trust. She didn't mind that. She trusted him to help her and Ava, to work to get them out of the situation safely.

She wasn't going to trust him with more than that.

Even if her heart skipped a beat and her cheeks warmed when she looked into his eyes. Even if she could see his integrity and kindness in everything he did and hear it in every word he said.

"There's a big difference between a large and sturdy puppy and a newborn," she pointed out. "But I appreciate the offer."

"That's a very polite way of saying you don't think I can be trusted with your child." He laughed, brushing dust from the cot and spreading a blanket over it. "How about you both lie down here, then?"

"I'm fine. Really."

"Suit yourself." He settled on the edge of the cot, back to the fire, hair deep black and glistening with the remnants of melting snow. "Tell me about Lance," he said, staring into her eyes as if he could see every secret she'd kept from Ariel—all the doubts she'd had near the end of the engagement, all the worries.

"What do you want to know?" she asked. Ava stirred, and she rubbed her back, enjoying the rhythmic movement of her daughter's breathing. Up until she'd found out she was pregnant, she had never thought about what it would be like to be a mother. She hadn't been all that interested in finding Mr. Right and settling down with him. Sure, she'd dated, but she had kept the relationships short and light.

She'd been in her midtwenties when her parents died. And hadn't been in any rush to find love.

There were too many gold diggers in the world, and she had no intention of being used by someone who only wanted her money. She'd gone to college, gotten a degree in business administration and had worked for her father's oil company. Nothing high-tech or glamorous. She'd been his assistant, and while it hadn't been fulfilling work, she'd enjoyed spending time with her dad. Eventually she had planned to open a nonprofit that helped underprivileged youth find jobs and attend college.

When her parents died, those plans had gone out the window.

She'd suddenly become CEO of her father's business and owner of three properties in Anchorage. Keeping up with everything had taken all her time and attention.

And then Lance had come along.

Visiting a friend of a friend.

Smiling at her at a dinner party hosted by one of her sorority sisters. He'd given her his number and told her to call. She'd been charmed enough to do it.

Worst mistake of her life…

"How likely is it that he'll stay out in weather like this?" Gabriel asked.

"Not very. He doesn't like to suffer. He likes to be comfortable, and he enjoys pursuits that don't take a lot of energy."

"Like?"

"Spending other people's money," she replied, despising the tinge of bitterness in her tone. Aside from the steel-cold edge of terror at the thought of him finding her, she no longer felt anything but apathy for Lance. But what she *did* feel was regret and shame for her actions and for the fact that she had been duped.

Gabriel watched impassively, his hair damp, the cut on his temple a dark slash on tan skin. He wore a police uniform, the shirt open at the collar, a black under layer visible.

Handsome.

Confident.

Quiet.

Watchful.

Violet shifted beneath his steady gaze, wishing he

would say something. Because she had nothing to add. No insight into why Lance had committed murder or why he seemed so determined to find her.

"If you want to know what motivates him," she finally said, "he likes nice things. Cars. Houses. He isn't as interested in people. Unless they can do something for him. I wish I had realized that before I got involved with him."

"I hope you aren't blaming yourself for what happened."

"I take responsibility for my part in it."

"What part? Being fooled by someone you loved? That's not your fault. It's his. You own no part of the guilt for that. It all belongs to Lance," Gabe said quietly, leaning forward so that his elbows were resting on his knees, his big, strong body just feet from hers.

She leaned toward him, somehow desperate for his strength and confidence, his kindness and warmth.

"That's nice of you to say, but it doesn't change how I feel," she murmured.

"Feelings are fickle, Violet. Facts are what matter, and the fact is, Lance is a criminal who uses people to get what he wants. He has made a habit of finding people who can payroll his hobbies. His sister has a lot to say about his skills as a manipulator and liar."

"That doesn't mean I should have fallen for him." She glanced down at Ava. She had gotten a beautiful little girl out of the relationship, but she still regretted it.

"Let's focus on the here and now, okay? The past is what it is. You can't change it, but you can make sure Lance doesn't hurt anyone again." He touched her hand, and warmth spread up her arm. Not the quick excitement she'd felt when she was around Lance. This was deeper, stronger and much more real. It was the kind of thing that lasted. She knew that as surely as she knew that the heartbreak she'd felt when she'd realized the truth about Lance was nothing compared to the heartbreak losing someone like Gabe would bring.

"You don't have to convince me to help you, Trooper Runyon," she said, trying to bring the conversation to a less personal level. She needed to steady herself before she did something she regretted. Like grabbing his hand and holding on to him like he was a lifeline in the raging storm of her life.

"Gabe," he corrected, glancing at Bear, who was sleeping beside the door. Jowls splayed on either side of his boxy head, snoring loudly enough that she could hear it above the sounds of the storm.

She couldn't help smiling.

"He seems to enjoy his downtime," she commented, wanting to turn the conversation away from her mistakes. He was correct. The past couldn't be changed. She needed to focus on the present. On getting through the storm and getting back to the bunker.

She frowned.

"You're not going to let me go back, are you?" she asked.

Gabe met her eyes. "No."

The answer was simple and direct.

No hedging. No pretending. No promises he didn't plan to keep.

"At least you're honest," she murmured, leaning her head back against the chair and closing her eyes.

"How about you be the same?" he suggested.

Her eyes flew open. "I have been."

"Do you want to go back to living in a bunker? Is that really where you plan to raise your daughter?"

"No, but until Lance is apprehended, it's the safest place for her."

"It *was* the safest place before you had the state police beside you," he responded. "I'm not going to let anything happen to you or your baby, Violet. I give you my word that Bear and I will do whatever it takes to keep you both safe."

It sounded good.

It sounded like everything she had been hoping for during her long months away from home—the police on her side, promising to make certain Lance didn't harm her or Ava.

But things that sounded good weren't always the case. She wouldn't trust blindly. Not again. There was too much at stake. Ava was depending on her to be smart and safe, and she would do anything for her daughter.

Even go back to hiding in the underground bunker. With or without Trooper Gabriel Runyon's permission.

The storm abated a few hours before dawn, the onslaught of snow and wind ceasing. Gabriel opened the back door and let Bear out, watching him bound through foot-high drifts, his huge body nimble and swift as he made a circuit around the area behind the cabin. Nose up, tail high, body relaxed, he made quick work of searching for trouble.

He found nothing.

That was a relief, but Gabe wasn't counting on things

staying quiet. If the suspicions of the K-9 team were correct, and if what little information Violet had shared was true, Lance had committed murder, colluded with Jared Dennis to kill Ariel and then spent the past seven months hunting Violet.

To silence her?

Seemed like a lot of effort to go through.

Especially because the K-9 team had made it clear that they wanted to question Lance and Jared in connection to not only Cal Brooks's homicide but also in regard to the double murder of that older couple in Anchorage who'd been slain during a home invasion/burglary.

If the men had been smart, they'd have left the area.

A successful business owner, Lance owned and operated an import-export business. He had plenty of connections who could have easily flown him out of Alaska.

But instead he'd stayed, going into hiding soon after the police had questioned him, claiming that he and Jared Dennis were afraid for their lives and hiding in a safe house until Violet was apprehended.

At first, the K-9 team had believed the story.

They'd been called to the scene of Cal Brooks's murder soon after the park police had discovered the crime scene. The wedding party had been slated to return from a wilderness tour. When they hadn't, park police had been called to search for them. They'd discovered the body of the tour guide but had lacked the resources for a canine search.

Alaska K-9 had been happy to help.

At the time it had seemed like a cut-and-dried case. Lance and his best man had called 911 from the safety of a cabin close to the park entrance. Jared had been shot in the arm—wounded, he claimed, by Violet. Gabe and his colleagues Hunter McCord and Maya Rodriguez had brought their dogs to the scene and undertaken a lengthy search of the area. They'd been certain they were hunting a killer, and they'd been anxious to get her in custody.

As weeks and months passed, they'd realized they might be looking for the terrified victim of a crime. They'd wondered if she'd survived, worried that she might not have. The dogs had worked Chugach State Park, searching for any sign that Violet was still alive. They'd found her cell phone and a diamond bracelet that Ariel said had been a wedding gift from Lance.

To Gabriel, it had looked like a gaudy piece of costume jewelry. Huge stones set in bright yellow gold. He'd been surprised to learn that it was worth tens of thousands of dollars. If he'd had that kind of money to spend on a woman, he would have purchased something a little more personal and a lot less ostentatious.

After Lance's refusal to turn himself in to the police for further questioning, the K-9 unit had subpoenaed his bank records. They'd discovered that his business was in the red and his condo was mortgaged to the hilt. He enjoyed the finer things in life, but he didn't seem to have the means to pay for it.

Marrying Violet would have changed all that.

As a matter of fact, the two had a joint bank account that they'd opened the day before they'd gone on the wilderness adventure. Close to two million dollars transferred into the account from Violet's trust funds. She had transferred most of it back out a few hours later.

Why?

Had she had misgivings?

Was she planning on backing out of the marriage?

Had that caused Lance to go on a murderous rampage that had ended in Cal Brooks's death? Those were questions Gabe needed to ask, but he hadn't had the heart to subject Violet to an aggressive interrogation. Not while they were hunkered down in a cold cabin, huddled near a fire trying to keep warm, and not while she seemed so exhausted.

She'd fallen asleep sitting in the chair, Ava held close to her heart. He'd let her sleep, allowed all the questions he needed to ask to simmer on the back burner. There would be time to ask them once he got her to safety.

"Is everything okay?" she asked.

He turned to face her, surprised at the way his heart jumped when he met her eyes. Ava was still in her arms, held snug against her shoulder, little hands fisted near a tiny perfect face.

He'd never been a baby kind of person. He preferred puppies. They were hardier and more predictable, in his opinion. But there was just something about this precious baby girl that made him melt. "Yes. Just had to let Bear out. He prefers the snow to the indoors."

"I guess if I had a fur coat like his, I'd do the same." She smiled tiredly. Looking more relaxed than she'd been the previous night, but obviously still on edge.

He didn't blame her.

Violet had been through a lot, and she'd survived it by staying hidden. Now she'd been discovered. Not just by the police, but also by a deranged man who seemed intent on harming her.

"Hopefully we'll get cell reception shortly. Now that the storm has cleared, the team should be able to deploy. We'll have you back in Anchorage by midday."

"I'm not sure that's the best thing for me and Ava," she said, patting the baby's back.

"No?"

"We've been safe because we've stayed hidden," Violet pointed out. "And if Ava and I go back to the Seavers', you can concentrate on apprehending Lance."

"You know I can't let you do that, right?" he asked, calling for Bear and closing the door after the dog walked inside.

"I don't remember asking permission." Her tone was haughty, but she looked scared.

"Violet, Lance followed you into the park. Which means he knows you're hiding somewhere out here. Do you really think he's going to stop searching now that he is certain you're still in the area?"

She didn't respond.

"I'll take that as a negative."

"You don't understand," she murmured.

"Then explain it to me. What's making you think you need to run from people who are trying to help?"

She was quiet for a moment, her hand smoothing down her daughter's tiny back. "Ava is my responsibility. I have to do what is best for her. If that means I spend another seven months in a bunker in the wilderness, that's what it means."

"We can put you in a safe house, Violet. The two of you will be well protected. There's no need to hide in a bunker, and the risk of Lance finding you has increased exponentially now that he knows you've been hiding in the park."

"The park is huge. There's no way he could track me through it," she responded, but he knew she was thinking about what he said.

Her expression was guarded, her body tense. He didn't want to push too hard, but he needed her to understand that he wasn't going to let her return to the bunker. It was too dangerous. His phone buzzed, and he looked at the screen. Hunter had sent a quick text. The team was on the way. "What's going on?" Violet asked nervously.

"The team is readying to deploy. They'll be here within the hour."

"I need to go." She hurried into the main room, grabbed her coat from the back of the chair and hurried into it.

"You know I can't let you leave, right?" he asked.

She froze, her hand on the strap of her pack. "I'm not under arrest, am I?"

"No, but you're wanted for questioning in regard to the murder of Cal Brooks."

"You already questioned me. I told you what I know."

"We need an official statement," he responded.

It was the truth.

More importantly, though, he needed to get her out of the wilderness and away from the imminent threat of Lance's return.

Gabe was armed. He would do whatever was necessary to protect Violet and her baby, but he would feel better surrounded by his colleagues. Men and women that he respected, trusted and counted on. "If I give my statement now, will you let me leave?" she asked.

He shot her a disbelieving look. "There is a foot of snow out there," he replied. "And you have a newborn."

"We'll manage." But she did peek out the window."

"You know that's not the best decision for your child. Bringing her out into the cold. Risking getting lost. Leaving obvious tracks for anyone to follow."

"Maybe you're right," she murmured, settling into the chair, seemingly exhausted. Her shoulders bowed, her face gaunt. Despite her natural beauty, she didn't look like any first-time mother he'd seen. No healthy glow. No excitement or enthusiasm.

She had lived in fear for months.

That had to have taken a toll.

He wanted to get her to safety, remove the threat that had been stalking her and then watch her bloom. Pink checks. Excitement. Joy. Those were the things he wanted for Violet.

"I'm not going to let anything happen to you or your baby," he promised.

"We're not your responsibility," she reminded him, but there was a catch in her voice that betrayed her fear. She was trying to be strong, but she was tired. He could see that, and he was going to do what he could to ease her burden and allow her the rest she so desperately needed.

His phone buzzed again. The team was on the move, heading into the park and following GPS coordinates to the cabin.

It wouldn't be long before backup arrived.

Gabe just had to keep Violet and her baby safe until then. That was his mission and his goal, and he wouldn't be satisfied that his job was done and done well until he knew the threats against them had been removed.

SIX

Violet was torn between excitement at the thought of returning to civilization and dread at the thought of what that would mean. She'd be back in her comfortable home with an oven, a refrigerator, a heater and fireplaces. Plenty of blankets and clothes. She could buy Ava a bassinet, a crib and all the little accoutrements that babies needed. But she'd also be easier to find. She hadn't been to town much, but on the few occasions when she'd risked it to get prenatal care, she'd bought newspapers and pored over articles that related to her disappearance.

The tragedy of her parents' deaths combined with the intrigue surrounding her disappearance had made her front-page news for a while. No doubt, when she reappeared, reporters would be vying for her story.

She could handle that. But what she truly worried about was Lance finding her.

He had chased her into the wilderness the day he'd murdered Cal Brooks, shouting that if he didn't catch her, the police would, and she would pay for the crimes she'd committed. Violet had no idea what he'd meant. She'd only known she had to escape him.

Now, after months of replaying the horrible events, she'd realized that Lance had planned everything. That he'd gone along with her wilderness adventure in order to get her alone, far away from help. The stories he had told the police—about her supposed affair with Cal, her violent rampage, her dash into the wilderness—had all been fabricated to make her look guilty. He hadn't intended for her to survive. He had probably planned to kill her and dump her body far from the scene of the crime, leaving it for scavengers.

All for what?

The two million dollars he had talked her into placing in a joint account?

She watched as Gabe walked to the window and looked outside. He seemed even taller than he had the previous day. Sunlight streaming through the window reflected off his badge and glimmered in his black hair. He had broad shoulders and lean muscles, and he seemed confident in his ability to stave off danger.

She hoped he was as capable as he was confident.

She thought he was. He had found her in a snowstorm, protected her and Ava through a long, cold night. He had made sure they were safe, even when that meant risking his life. That was something she could respect and believe in and trust.

"You okay?" Gabe asked.

He had turned to face her, his eyes vivid blue. Handsome, fit and at ease with himself, he was the sort of guy most women would take a second look at.

Violet was no exception, but she had fallen for another handsome face. She had no intention of ever making that mistake again.

"I want this to be over," she admitted. "I want to move on with my life and put this behind me and make a good life for my daughter."

He nodded. "I can understand that, and I'm going to do everything I can to make certain it happens, but you're going to have to cooperate with us."

"I wasn't planning to do anything else," she assured him, shifting Ava so that the baby was cradled in her arms. Wispy blond hair peeked out from beneath a cap Dana Seavers had knit. Yellow and white with little snowflake patterns in it.

"I'm glad to hear that." He dragged the trunk over and sat in in front of her, perched on the old wood, his intense gaze locked on her face. "Maybe you can help us understand what Lance wants. He has resources available that would make it easy for him to leave Alaska, so why did he stay? What is his goal?"

"Aside from killing me because I ruined his plans?" She shivered and pulled a wool blanket tighter around her shoulders.

"He's risking a lot for revenge. If he's caught, he's going to spend his life in prison. There has to be something more," he prodded.

"Money. We opened a joint account the day before we went on our wilderness tour. We were going to buy a property in Miami. Lance had made a cash offer and wanted the money to come from a mutual account. We planned to honeymoon in Miami and close the deal while we were there."

He didn't speak, and she was certain he was processing the information, trying to decide how much validity it had. "Is that the account that had money transferred out in the early morning the day of the murders?"

"Yes."

"Was Lance aware that the money was no longer available to him?"

She hesitated, almost embarrassed to admit that she'd had suspicions but had planned to go through with the wedding anyway. "Not that I'm aware of. If he had been, he would have confronted me about it."

"So, he had two million reasons to think he could escape Alaska after the murders," he said as much to himself as to her.

She nodded. "I've had plenty of time to think about it, and I'm sure that was his plan. What I'm not entirely sure of is if he went out there planning to kill Cal, or if something happened that made him think he *had* to do it. Either way, he was expecting to leave Anchorage with the money and, probably, without me."

"My suspicion is that he never planned to kill anyone. He probably planned to skip town with the money and start a new life somewhere. Criminal and malicious, but not a crime that could get him tossed in jail for life. Jared was probably in on that plan, and Cal may have overheard them discussing things. It's possible he threatened to go to you with the truth, and they killed him because of that." The words were mater-of-fact, his expression neutral. This was the kind of thing he dealt with all the time, but it was new to Violet. The betrayal still hurt. The depth of Lance's depravity still made her shudder.

"You broke that down nicely, Gabe. It sounds very

neat and tidy. No emotion or betrayal behind it. If only it felt that way," she murmured.

"I'm sorry. I didn't mean to sound cold."

"You didn't. I'm just… I guess I still can't believe Lance could be so evil."

"I'm sorry. You deserved better." He touched her arm, looked into her eyes, made her feel as if she were a victim rather than a fool who had gotten what she deserved.

"I should have been more careful. If I make it through this—"

"You will."

"I'm going to spend the rest of my life raising Ava to be the strong, independent and confident woman I wasn't. With the right tools, she should be able to avoid getting herself into this kind of trouble."

"You're carrying a lot of blame for something that wasn't your fault," he commented, his gaze shifting as Bear lumbered to his feet.

"You've said something similar before, and I know you're right. I couldn't have predicted any of this, and I couldn't have known Lance was using me, but I still feel like a fool."

"He was the fool. You're a strong, intelligent, beautiful woman. He obviously was too blind to realize that he was giving up the real prize in exchange for monetary reward." His gaze returned to her, and he smiled, the sweet curve of his lips making her pulse race.

"That's a nice thing to say."

"*Nice* is not an adjective most people would use to describe me. Honest, honorable, driven. Those are my things." He touched her cheek, his fingers tracing a line to her jaw. "So, take what I said for what it's worth, and know that I wouldn't say it unless I absolutely believed it. Lance was a fool, and if I had been in his shoes, I'd have spent every day of my life proving just how wonderful you are and how worthy of affection, love and respect." His hand slipped away, but the warmth of his fingers lingered.

Bear growled, breaking the sudden silence. Head cocked, eyes focused on the door, the dog growled again, the fur on his nape standing up.

"What's wrong? Is someone out the—" she began, but Gabe put a finger to his lips, cautioning her to stay quiet.

"Listen," he whispered.

She did, waiting in the silence, her heart thundering in her chest.

At first, she heard nothing but the quiet rasp of her breath and Bear's low growl. Then, another sound drifted into the cabin. An engine rumbling in the distance.

"Is that your team?" she asked, terrified that it wasn't and that Lance was back.

"I don't think so," he replied. "Stay here."

He was up and in his coat before she could think to question his plans. Leather gloves on his hands. Bear by his side. "I'll be back soon. Don't leave the cabin," he cautioned as he stepped outside with the St. Bernard and closed the door.

She wanted to call him back, but the words stuck in her throat, terror making her mute.

If she hadn't had Ava to think about, she might have gone out the back door and run. She had a head start and knew she wasn't far from the bunker. But the snow was deep. Her tracks would be easy to follow, and she didn't dare bring danger into the lives of people who had helped her.

So she stayed where she was, huddled beneath a blanket, holding Ava close and praying that Lance would be stopped before anyone else was hurt.

Gabe sent a text to Hunter McCord asking for an update on the team's ETA. It was possible they had made excellent time and were closing in on the cabin, but he expected them to be farther out. If they were, someone else was approaching in a snowmobile.

As the engine roared closer, he made his way up a nearby hill and studied the landscape, searching for signs of the vehicle. Bear stood beside him, body alert, tail up. His K-9 partner had his face to the west, and Gabe focused his attention there. There was a trail in that direction—a hiking and biking path that wound through the park and around Eklutna Lake. Anyone familiar with the area would know of it.

As he watched, two snowmobiles came into view. Just specks of black against the pristine white trail. He couldn't make out details, but the team would have more manpower with it.

Bear growled again, his muzzle lifted to the air.

"I see them, buddy," Gabe assured him.

His phone buzzed, and he checked the message. The team was still twenty minutes out. But the two snowmobilers would be on them in ten. *If* they were heading for the cabin.

He typed a quick message, giving what little information he had about the vehicles, still watching the dark specks curving around the icy blue water of the lake. Maybe they were nature lovers out for a snow-day ride.

The lead snowmobile turned off the path, disappearing into the trees and heading in the direction of the cabin. The second vehicle followed.

His adrenaline spiked.

"Not what I wanted to see," he muttered, updating Hunter and hurrying back inside.

Violet was where he had left her, sitting in the chair, a blanket over her shoulders. The fire had died down, the flames eating at the wood he had tossed in earlier.

"Is everything okay?" she asked, standing up and grabbing her pack from the floor. She pulled out the baby sling and tried to put it on while still holding Ava.

"Someone is heading this way," he said.

She froze, the sling dropping from her hands, her face pale beneath layers of thick tan makeup. "Not your team?"

"No. We need to be prepared to take off at a moment's notice."

"You'll get no argument from me!" she said, reaching for the sling again and fumbling to get into it one-handed.

"I can take the baby," he offered without thinking. He wanted to expedite the process and get Violet ready to run, if they had to. But holding her baby was honestly the last thing he wanted to do.

She hesitated, looking into his eyes, her expression still guarded but so filled with fear, that he had the urge to pull her into his arms and assure her that everything was going to be okay.

"You have to support her head," she said quietly. "She's still too young to do it herself."

He nodded.

In theory, he knew what she meant. He had friends with kids. He'd even helped out in the church nursery a few times when it was understaffed and in need of an extra set of hands. But he had always avoided newborns.

He knew nothing about them. Except that they were completely helpless, completely dependent and absolutely fragile.

When Violet passed Ava to him, the swaddled bundle of tiny humanity fitting into the crook of his arm, he looked into the baby's face. Found himself drinking in her soft cheeks and pink lips, her closed eyes and one miniature fist that had escaped the blanket.

His heart jumped. A quick thud of fear and wonder and worry. This innocent child was out in the wilderness being hunted by her own father. A man who had killed once and would not hesitate to kill again.

Ava was being raised in an underground bunker away from medical help and friendships and sunlit windows. She deserved better. Gabe had felt protective of many things and many people during his time as an Alaska state trooper. He had a deep desire to see justice done and to protect the innocent, but he had never felt such an intense need to shelter someone, to hide them from the world and to make certain that nothing ugly or mean ever touched them.

"I'm done," Violet said, reaching for the baby.

He handed Ava back, that fierce need to protect still lodged deeply in his heart.

The snowmobiles had stopped, the engines silenced.

He imagined Lance and his lackey, Jared, hiking closer, trying to be surreptitious in their approach. Silent predators stalking their prey.

"Are we leaving now?" Violet asked, Ava already in the sling, her coat on. She zipped it so that only the baby's tiny knit cap was visible.

"I was planning to leave, but I think it's better to have walls around us if Lance is close," he responded, pulling his focus away from the baby and meeting Violet's dark blue eyes.

"Walls don't keep out bullets."

"No, but they'll offer some protection," he replied, sliding into his pack and helping Violet into hers. "My team isn't very far out. They're aware that Lance and Jared may be nearby, and if we stay here, that will give them an opportunity to move in on Lance and Jared."

"Jared is out there, too?" She glanced at the window, the fear in her eyes belying her calm tone.

"I saw two snowmobiles. If Lance is on one, Jared is on the other."

She nodded, her hand dropping to the baby's back, the protective gesture touching him to the core. He had interviewed enough people to know when someone was being honest. What little she had said had rung true.

She was an innocent victim in this. The woman's only "crime"? Being duped by a man she loved.

"I'm sorry for what you've been through, Violet. I know it's been tough, but we're almost on the other side of it. You're going to get back to your old life and to normalcy. You're going to be safe again," he vowed.

"I hope you're right," she replied, her voice catching on the last word. As if she had used up every bit of faith she had, as if hope were a fragile snow-covered blossom, waiting for the sun to bring it to life.

Bear barked, the sound jolting Ava.

She wailed, a kitten-like cry that startled Bear into silence. He padded to Violet, gently nosing her coat, sniffing Ava's hat and head.

Violet didn't back up. She didn't ask Gabe to call off the dog. Instead, she merely watched as Bear nosed Ava's cheek. The baby stopped crying, and Bear retreated, rushing to the door and pawing frantically at the wood.

"Is someone out there?" Violet asked. This time, he could hear the anxiety in her voice.

She was backing into the other room, probably trying to get closer to an escape route.

"Yes," he responded honestly.

There was no sense in trying to hide the truth.

"Is it Lance?"

"I think we're about to find out," he replied tersely. "Stay away from the windows and stay low."

She nodded, dropping to her knees, one hand supporting Ava as she crawled to the threshold of the back room.

A gunshot exploded, the window shattering, cold air sweeping in.

Not an attempt to kill.

A warning, perhaps?

"Come on out of there, Violet!" a man yelled. "Unless you want your new friend and his dog to get hurt."

"Lance," she mouthed, her pulse pounding frantically in the hollow of her throat. He could see it there, beating beneath pale skin.

He moved closer, whispered in her ear, "We just have to hold him off for a few minutes. The team will be here soon. See if you can engage him in conversation."

She nodded. "Go home, Lance. Leave me alone!" she called, her voice shaking but her tone firm.

"Honey, why would you want me to do something like that? We're going to spend our lives together, remember?" he crooned.

"You're a cold-blooded murderer! I want nothing to do with you."

"Well, now, isn't that a shame. After all the times you claimed to love me, you're going to abandon me in my hour of need?"

"You tried to kill me."

"If I'd tried, you'd be dead. A little poison in your morning coffee, dump your body in the lake—it would have been done." He nearly spat the words.

Gabe eased toward the window, hoping to get a good visual and a good shot. If he had to, he would take Lance out. He was prepared to do whatever it took to protect Violet and Ava.

"You know what your problem is, darling," Lance said. "You lack vision. Your parents did you the favor of dying and leaving you with a fortune, and you spend your days sitting in a musty office running a company that you could sell for billions of dollars. Me? I'd have taken the money and retired. As a matter of fact, I *was* planning to take the money and retire. That cool two million was my ticket out of here. I was heading to Bangkok. You ruined that."

Gabe made it to the window and motioned for Violet to keep talking. Bear was still near the front door, whining softly and scratching the wood. Gabe signaled for him to heel, and the dog joined him, glued to his left side.

"You lied about everything, didn't you?" Violet demanded. "You never cared about me. You never loved me."

"Of course I didn't. Did you really think someone like me would want someone like you? You're a mousy little girl with no interests outside of books and business. The only thing exciting about you is your money."

Gabe scowled, the urge to climb out the window and shut Lance up so strong, he had to remind himself that Lance hadn't come alone and that flying off the handle would accomplish nothing.

Logic and careful planning trumped emotional responses.

Always.

He'd learned that while growing up in foster care. Gabe had had no one to show him how to be an adult. He hadn't had anyone invested enough in his life to teach him what it meant to have emotional control. And instead had to learn through trial and error, a ton of mistakes and missteps.

He eased to the window ledge, peered out into the bright day. As he suspected, Lance was just feet away, a shotgun resting against his shoulder. He wasn't planning to let Violet out of this alive.

And even though he couldn't see Jared, he knew the guy was out there, too.

Gabriel pulled his firearm, prepared to draw Jared out by threatening Lance.

"Freeze!" he called. "Police!"

Lance jumped back, stumbling in his haste to duck behind a tree.

"Now!" he shouted.

A soft pop followed his command.

For a moment nothing happened.

Then the door exploded in flames, smoke billowing up to the rafters, fire lapping at the old log walls.

Violet screamed, jumping to her feet and running to the back door. He caught her before she could open it.

"Don't!" he said. "That's what they're expecting."

"We have to get out!" she cried, her hand on the latch.

"We will, but we're not going out the door." He took her arm, hurrying her back to the window where Lance had been standing.

Footprints were clearly visible in the snow, leading from the trees toward the back of the cabin. They were waiting there, probably hoping to kill Gabe and take Violet and Ava alive.

He gestured for her to wait, then climbed silently through the window, making sure there were no shards of glass. Bear followed, bounding out with little effort. In the distance, engines roared, the sound of backup arriving filling Gabe with relief. Soon the men and women he trusted most would be there to help.

His coworkers. The only real family he had ever known. He reached for Violet, helping her navigate through the window, then pulling her into a full-out run toward the trees. Bear turned his head, growling ferociously as a shadow appeared at the corner of the cabin.

Gabe didn't hesitate.

He fired.

The person dropped with a howl of pain.

Gabe kept moving, running into the trees, Violet beside him, Bear on his heels. The sound of engines was growing louder. The team was getting closer. He just needed to hold the perps back until help arrived.

SEVEN

Violet raced into the woods, Ava tucked securely in the sling under her coat. Fabric wouldn't protect her from a bullet. Love couldn't keep her from being hurt or worse. But as she pushed through knee-deep snow, Violet prayed that she and her baby would survive this ordeal as she unconsciously began moving in the direction of the bunker.

Gabe's hand was on her wrist, his fingers tight as he tried to steer her downhill toward Eklutna Lake. She changed course, forcing herself to ignore the knee-jerk desire to return to the one place she had felt safe during her pregnancy.

She didn't want the Seavers hurt. Didn't dare bring trouble to their doorstep. Not in the form of Lance or the police. If she was going to return, she'd have to be very careful about how she did it. *If* she was going to return. She craved safety and security. That, more than anything, was what home meant to her, and it was where she longed to be.

"Get down!" Gabe yelled, yanking her behind a tree. Moments later, a bullet slammed into the trunk, bark ricocheting into the snow. Violet winced, her arms crossing over Ava's tiny back. She had an obligation to protect her daughter, a duty to keep her safe, and she would do anything necessary to accomplish that.

Gabe hurried to a pile of deadfall and urged her to stay down.

Violet curled up on her side, desperate to shield Ava. The downed trees were nearly two feet high, but even that couldn't keep them safe from flying bullets.

Her eyes darted toward the trooper, and she saw he had his firearm drawn and was peering through cracks between dead branches. Someone was calling for help, shouting that he had been shot and needed an ambulance. Not Lance. She knew his voice as well as she knew her own.

It had to be Jared.

"Put your weapons down!" Gabe shouted. "Now!"

"Violet, I don't want to hurt anyone, but if you don't come out here and give me what I want, I won't be responsible for my actions," Lance responded. He sounded closer than she'd expected. Yards away, maybe, waiting for Violet or Gabe to lift their heads.

She didn't respond, didn't move. Bear was beside her, his big head close, his gaze focused on his partner. "I said, drop the weapon," Gabriel demanded.

"I did!" Jared hollered back. "I'm unarmed. Please, I need help. I'm going to bleed to death."

"It's a flesh wound, you idiot," Lance snapped. "Pull yourself together."

"We'll get you the help you need. Step out where I can see you. Hands up," Gabe called.

"Don't be a coward," Lance growled. "Violet, come

on out and let me see my baby. Boy or girl? I need to know how to decorate the nursery when I leave town."

She bit her lip, refusing to be baited into speaking.

Lance wasn't father material. Trusting him, *loving* him, had been terrible mistakes. She wanted to believe she was smarter and wiser now, no longer the sheltered and naive young woman who had been swept off her feet by charming words and focused attention.

"Cat got your tongue, baby?" he called. "Or is your new buddy calling the shots like I always did? He says jump, you jump. He says hide, you hide. He says keep your mouth shut, and you do?"

She glanced at Gabe.

He seemed unfazed, his focus never wavering, his gun aimed in the direction of Lance's voice. She had never known anyone like him—someone who could face down a threat without flinching, a man willing to sacrifice himself for a stranger.

She wanted to thank him now, just in case there wasn't a chance later, but she didn't dare speak.

"I can forgive you for betraying me, babe," Lance continued. "We can still have the life we planned together. We can take our baby and leave Alaska together. Just the three of us. A happy little family. That's what you wanted, right?"

He knew it was.

She had poured her heart out to him, reveling in the attention he had given. Thinking about it made her cheeks heat and her stomach churn.

After her parents died, she had been desperate for connectivity. She had craved the comfort of family bonds. Her mother and father had been older, both of them only children. Her arrival had surprised and delighted them. They had given her love and time, but they hadn't been able to give her siblings or cousins, uncles or aunts. Their friends were their family.

In the distance a dog barked.

"Last warning," Gabe called. "Put down your weapons and step out where I can see you. Hands up. No sudden moves."

"Please, help me!" Jared cried once again.

"I said *shut up*," Lance screamed.

The boom of a gunshot followed.

Then silence.

The dog had stopped barking, and the world seemed to be holding its breath. Even the trees seemed to have stopped rustling.

Violet shifted, terrified of what it meant.

Gabe inched closer, his shoulder warm against hers, his presence as comforting as dawn after the darkest, longest night. She had felt alone for so long, she had forgotten what it felt like to be together. Gabe made her feel that—as if she were part of something more than just herself. Two people facing trouble together were more powerful than one person alone.

She felt that to her bones as Bear dropped his big head on her legs, the warmth of his muzzle seeping through fabric and into her chilled skin.

"Violet! Get out here. Now!"

There was an edge to Lance's voices, a frantic energy that she had never heard before.

Bear barked in return, the dog shifting his attention downhill.

She did the same, surprised to see a Siberian husky darting through the trees, heading straight for them.

Another shot was fired, this one slamming into a tree a dozen yards away.

"He's on the move," Gabriel said, and she realized he had his phone in hand and was speaking to someone. "Heading west. Probably back to his snowmobile." He slipped the phone in his pocket.

"Stay here," he said. "A trooper is just below us. He'll be here shortly."

He gave Bear a command to stay, then jumped over the deadfall and took off.

Should she make a run for the bunker? She shifted onto an elbow, her free arm wrapped around Ava as she peered between dead branches. A man lay on blood-stained snow, arms and legs splayed. Gabe paused beside him, touching his wrist and neck before moving on.

Was it Jared lying dead in the snow? She couldn't make out details. Wasn't sure she wanted to. Violet had never liked Jared. She'd thought he was crass and seedy, and she'd often wondered how a charming person like Lance could be friends with him.

Now she understood that they were cut from the same cloth, and that Lance was the worse of the two—hiding his true colors beneath a coat of manners and civility. Jared had been his lackey, doing what he was told and following blindly.

She hadn't liked him, but she certainly hadn't wanted him dead.

Bear lifted his head, his gaze still on the husky.

It darted toward them, rushing in to sniff Violet's

hair before running off again. Minutes later, she heard a man yell, "Good job! Show me!"

Two police officers appeared, running after the husky and heading straight toward Violet.

She stayed down and quiet as they reached her.

"Ma'am, I'm Trooper Hunter McCord. This is my colleague, Trooper Maya Rodriguez. She's going to escort you down to our ATVs and get you back to civilization."

"Gabe is still out here. I can't leave without him," Violet said, her voice thick with nerves. She wasn't used to being around people, and her communication skills felt rusty. Aside from the Seavers and a few medical professionals, she hadn't spoken to anyone until Gabe had found her the previous day. They had been a team all night, working together to stay warm and safe.

She wouldn't leave him behind.

She couldn't.

"We have several officers joining him. He's going to be fine," Trooper Rodriguez said kindly, her gaze shifting from Violet's face to Ava's head. "It's cold, though, and we've got another storm blowing in soon. Let's get you and your baby inside and warm."

She offered a hand.

Violet hesitated. "I can't leave him out here."

"Do you really think he would want you and the baby to stay in the cold waiting?" Trooper Rodriguez asked.

He wouldn't.

Violet knew that.

She took the offered hand, allowing herself to be pulled to her feet. Bear stayed down, head resting on his paws, not the least bit concerned about the commotion that was going on around him. "What about the dog?" she asked.

As if on cue, someone whistled. Bear jumped up, bounded over the deadfall and ran.

"Gabe just whistled. Bear will make quick work of reuniting with him," Trooper Rodriguez reassured her, turning her head as another dog ran out from between trees. "Sarge! Heel," she called.

The K-9 immediately took a position on her left.

"I'm heading out. Radio if you have any trouble," Trooper McCord said, hurrying away, the husky by his side.

"Ready?" the female trooper asked, meeting Violet's eyes. She had a kind face and an easy smile. Maybe that was why she'd been chosen to escort Violet out of the park.

"Yes," Violet responded, but she wasn't sure she was.

She had been dreaming about this moment for months, praying about it, begging God to allow her to return to civilization and her life. But now that it was happening, she didn't feel ready. She'd been away for too long, had lived with a family she'd grown to love. And now she was leaving everything she had known, everything that had kept her safe, and walking into the unknown.

Violet sighed. She had no idea what the police were thinking. For all she knew, she was still a suspect in Cal's murder and they were going to take her to jail and toss her in a cell.

She must have looked as anxious and unsure as she felt.

"Everything is going to be okay," Trooper Rodriguez said as she and her dog headed down the hill.

Violet followed, a feeling of finality and sorrow filling her. She was saying goodbye to the survivalist lifestyle, carrying all the lessons she had learned and heading back home.

To a new beginning.

A fresh start.

She and Ava. The two of them facing the world together.

"It's going to be fine," she whispered, patting Ava's back and praying that she was right and that the police would apprehend Lance. That he would be put in prison and that he would stay there.

He had killed Cal, and he had shot his best friend. Probably killed him, too.

Why? To shut him up? To keep him from turning himself in? Whatever the case, Lance's actions proved what Violet had already known—he was a very dangerous man. One without a conscience and without a heart. If he found her again, if he had the opportunity, he would kill her.

I forgive you for betraying me, babe.

He certainly hadn't been talking about her relationship with Cal. There hadn't been one. Maybe he had been putting on an act for Gabe's benefit.

Or, maybe, he was talking about the money she had transferred from their account. Money he would have had access to while she was hiding in the bunker. Money that would have made his escape easy. She'd taken it from him.

Probably worse in his mind, she had stepped out from under his control and done something he hadn't anticipated. Their relationship had always been about him. What he wanted and needed. What he felt and believed. She had worked hard to be the woman he wanted, jumping through every hoop he had set in front of her because she had been afraid to lose him. And he had probably firmly believed that would never change.

She had fooled him, and he couldn't forgive that. Now he wanted to make her pay. She shuddered, hurrying to keep up with Trooper Rodriguez.

It was time to leave Chugach State Park. Time to face the police. Time to do whatever it took to make sure Lance never hurt anyone again.

She glanced back, hoping to catch a glimpse of Gabe. He had stepped in and helped when she'd needed it most, and he was sacrificing his safety for her and Ava's sake. She wanted to thank him. She needed to tell him just how much she appreciated the safety he'd provided and the kind words he had offered. More than anything, she wanted to tell him to be careful. She couldn't bear the thought of anything happening to him, but he was gone, swallowed up by the forest and heading back into danger.

Gabe followed Lance's tracks through the snow, Bear loping a few meters ahead, both of them flanked by other K-9 teams. Helena Maddox and her dog, Luna, to their left. Will Stryker and his dog, Scout, to their right.

Of the three K-9s, Luna would be the most useful in this situation. Trained in apprehension, she would track Lance and take him down as soon as she was given the command.

"You want me to send her ahead?" Helena asked, her gaze focused on her dog. They were a great team.

Tough and no-nonsense. Always ready to do what it took to capture suspects.

"He rode in on a snowmobile. I'm worried about him running over Luna if she gets too close," he responded.

"Luna doesn't let anyone get the best of her," Will said.

He was right. The Norwegian elkhound was sweet and accommodating when she wasn't working. When she was on the job, she was ferocious.

"It's your call, Helena. She's your partner."

She nodded, then gave Luna the command to work.

Luna took off, shooting into the woods and disappearing from view. Seconds later, a snowmobile motor roared to life. Lance had reached his escape vehicle. Gabe knew Luna was fast, but not fast enough to chase it down. "I'm calling in for park rangers to be on the lookout for a snowmobiler," Will said. "You want to let Maya and Hunter know he might head down to the road?"

"He'd be an idiot to do that," Helena muttered.

"He shot a man in front of me. I wouldn't give him high points for intelligence," Gabe muttered.

He hadn't expected Lance to shoot his best friend in cold blood, and he regretted not pulling the trigger and firing into the trees. Unfortunately, he hadn't had a clear line of sight, and firing blindly was a good way to get an innocent person killed. So he'd waited, hoping to catch a clear view and bring Lance down.

Waiting had cost Jared his life.

"Don't beat yourself up, Gabe," Will said as if he could read his mind and knew his thoughts.

Maybe he could, and maybe he did.

They were a family built by their strong desires to protect and serve the community. There wasn't a member of the team who didn't value every human life. Jared was a criminal, but his crimes should have been judged by a jury of his peers, his punishment decided by a court of law.

"I should have tried to take Lance out."

"Did you have a clear shot?" Will asked.

"No."

"Then you did the right thing. If Jared didn't want to be shot and killed by his best friend, he should have chosen a better one."

"Lance is a loose cannon, and he needs to be apprehended," Helena added. "He's unpredictable and dangerous, and as long as he is free, the community isn't safe."

"I'd like to know why he's hanging around. He could have flown out of Alaska seven months ago and left us chasing down Violet, thinking she was the prime suspect in the Brooks murder." Will whistled for Scout. The border collie rushed to his side. Small and nimble, Scout was trained in narcotics detection.

"Money is my guess," Gabe replied. "The joint account that was opened and then emptied out the night before the wilderness excursion? That may be key. I suspect he planned to leave town with the cash either before or after the wedding."

"And found out there was no money to leave with?" Helena asked.

"I'm not sure if he found out before or after the shooting," Gabe admitted. "Violet wasn't in the mood to talk, and I didn't want to press her for too many answers when she was taking care of a baby."

"I understand," Helena said. "But the sooner we ask the hard questions, the sooner we'll have a clear picture of what is driving Lance. He could have left Alaska months ago, but he's stayed. Why? What is he hoping to achieve? Once we know that, we'll be able to stop him."

"Money?" he suggested. "Violet said material possessions are his motivating factor."

"If that's the case," Will cut in, "and Lance was planning to empty the account, leave town before the wedding and live off the two million, it's possible Brooks overheard them talking about their plans."

"And was killed to ensure his silence? Just about anything is possible, but I think you may be on to something," Gabe responded. "Two million dollars can buy a really nice lifestyle in South America. Lance has his pilot's license and access to a plane. We already know that his business was deeply in the red, that he was tens of thousands of dollars in debt and that his condo was going into foreclosure."

"So he preyed on a vulnerable woman and planned to rob her blind, then killed a man to make sure she didn't find out? Nice guy," Helena muttered.

"I sure wouldn't want him on my friend list," Gabe said.

"I wouldn't want him on my enemy list, either. The guy has no conscience. He shot his best friend dead. I can't imagine what he'd do to someone he didn't like." Will shook his head.

"Stalk her for months? Make her live in fear? Try to kill someone she loves?" Helena suggested.

"Kidnap her baby, if he has the chance," Gabe added, every cell in his body rebelling at the thought of a thug like Lance getting his hands on Ava. She was fragile and tiny, and the thought of anyone hurting her made his blood boil.

The sound of the snowmobile's engine had faded to a muted rumble, and he bit back a groan of frustration. "I think he's managed to escape again."

"He can't run forever. Eventually we'll catch him and make him pay for what he's done." Helena called for Luna.

Minutes later, the elkhound appeared, glossy black against the bright white snow.

Clouds were moving in again, crowding close to the sun. More snow was arriving. Winter was just around the corner. And soon the park would be more difficult to travel. Would Lance finally give up and leave Anchorage? Or would he stay for as long as it took to accomplish his goal? Without his lackey, he might not have the guts to stick things out, but he'd proven to be a masterful manipulator and a seasoned liar. He'd almost had the K-9 team convinced that he and Jared were victims of Violet's violent rampage.

After months of interviewing her friends, coworkers and acquaintances, Gabe was certain Violet had too much compassion and empathy to hurt anyone.

She and her daughter needed to be protected.

He felt compelled to be the one to do it. He had looked into Violet's eyes. He had seen the fear and the strength there. She would do what it took to keep her baby safe, and he was determined to stand beside her, fight with her and make certain they both survived until Lance was caught and tossed in jail.

If that meant twenty-four-hour security, that's what she'd get. Gabe had assured Violet that everything would be okay. He intended to make certain it was. No matter what it took, no matter how many hours, he would find Lance and he would toss him behind bars where he belonged. Violet and her baby deserved to have peace in their lives, and he would do whatever it took to make certain they got it.

EIGHT

Violet expected to be taken to the Anchorage police department, and she had braced herself for an intense interrogation.

Instead, she had been transported to the federal building. The white facade gleamed in muted sunlight as she was hurried inside and up a flight of stairs. Offices lined the long hallway of the historic building, and she could hear the normal sounds of busy office life.

It felt odd to be there, a trooper flanking her to either side, two dogs padding beside them. Life in the Seavers' bunker had become normal, whereas the hubbub of Anchorage life had become strange. Electric lights. Gleaming floors. Heat chugging out of ceiling vents. She felt overwhelmed and overstimulated, and she worried that Ava would feel the same.

She patted the baby's back as she was led into a small conference room.

"Violet, if you'll have a seat, we'll have someone with you shortly. We have a few questions to ask before we release you to return home," Trooper Rodriguez said. Tall and slender, she held the lead of a small Ma-

Get up to 4
FREE FABULOUS BOOKS
You Love!

To thank you for being a loyal reader we'd like to send you up to 4 FREE BOOKS, absolutely free.

Just write "YES" on the Loyal Reader Voucher and we'll send you up to 4 Free Books and Free Mystery Gifts, altogether worth over $20, as a way of saying thank you for being a loyal reader.

Try **Love Inspired® Romance Larger-Print** books and fall in love with inspirational romances that take you on an uplifting journey of faith, forgiveness and hope.

Try **Love Inspired® Suspense Larger-Print** books where courage and optimism unite in stories of faith and love in the face of danger.

Or **TRY BOTH!**

We are so glad you love the books as much as we do and can't wait to send you great new books.

So don't miss out, return your Loyal Reader Voucher Today!

Pam Powers

LOYAL READER
FREE BOOKS VOUCHER

YES! I Love Reading, please send me up to 4 FREE BOOKS and Free Mystery Gifts from the series I select.

Just write in "YES" on the dotted line below then return this card today and we'll send your free books & gifts asap!

➡ YES ⬅

Which do you prefer?

| ☐ **Love Inspired®**
Romance
Larger-Print
122/322 IDL GRJD | ☐ **Love Inspired®**
Suspense
Larger-Print
107/307 IDL GRJT | ☐ **BOTH**
122/322 & 107/307
IDL GRJP |

FIRST NAME	LAST NAME

ADDRESS

APT.#	CITY

STATE/PROV.	ZIP/POSTAL CODE

EMAIL ☐ Please check this box if you would like to receive newsletters and promotional emails from Harlequin Enterprises ULC and its affiliates. You can unsubscribe anytime.

linois that looked like it was still a puppy. She looked as relaxed inside the building as she had out in the woods, confidence and kindness seeping out in everything she did.

"Do I need to call an attorney?" Violet asked. Her father had always had lawyers on the payroll, and he had never been afraid to utilize their services. He had lived his life with integrity and purpose, but running a multibillion-dollar company often made him a target of false accusations and lawsuits.

Trooper Rodriguez frowned, her dark eyes spearing into Violet's. "If you feel the need to have an attorney present while you're being questioned, that is your prerogative."

"Am I being questioned because I'm a suspect in a crime?" she asked. That was another skill she had learned from her father—don't be afraid to ask questions. You can't formulate good plans of action without accurate and complete information. Without those things, you were just fumbling around in the dark.

"You're being questioned as a witness to the murder of Cal Brooks and the attempted murder of Ariel Potter," the trooper said. "But, like I said, if you want an attorney present, you're welcome to call one."

"I don't have a phone," she pointed out.

"We can bring you one. Have a seat. Do you want coffee? Tea? Cocoa? Something to eat?"

"No, thanks."

The trooper nodded and stepped into the corridor. "I'll be back shortly."

She shut the door, leaving Violet and Ava alone.

There were windows on the far side of the room,

and Violet opened the shades, letting muted sunlight filter in. Clouds dotted the horizon, another storm on the way. She had weathered several spring storms in the bunker, snow and rain and cold making life in the wilderness even more complicated.

The Seavers had their lives down to a science.

They knew when to plant, reap and harvest, knew how much meat they would need for long winter seasons, and they went to town every couple of months to trade fur and leather for supplies.

Violet admired them, and she appreciated everything they had taught her, but she hadn't wanted to spend her life off the grid. She liked being in touch with friends. She liked going to the office every day, returning home to a warm house and comfortable furniture. The Seavers' seventeen-year-old son, Harrison, felt the same. When his parents had made the decision to go off the grid, he had been old enough to have strong memories of living in a house, enjoying modern conveniences. He had admitted to Violet that, while he enjoyed the outdoors and appreciated the survival skills he had, he wanted to return to civilization, attend college and go into veterinary medicine. She knew he was smart enough to do it and had secretly planned to help.

After all his parents had done for her, the least she could do was pay for him to pursue his dreams.

The door opened, and a young man stepped in. Tall and lanky with dark hair, he wore jeans, a gray button-down shirt and a bright blue vest.

"Ms. James?" he asked, pushing round black glasses up his nose and smiling.

"Yes."

"I'm Eli Partridge. I work tech for the Alaska K-9 unit. I heard you needed a phone." He placed a cell phone on the table. "You can use this one. We have landlines, but we think it's best if you stay in here until we get a handle on what's going on with Lance."

"Thank you," she murmured, staying near the window.

She felt skittish and unsure. An odd development, as she had always been confident in social settings. Violet might have been a loner, but her parents had always included her in social gatherings and events. She had learned to be at ease no matter where she was.

Seven months in a bunker away from civilization seemed to have changed that.

"No problem." He crossed his arms and shifted his weight, staring at her intently.

"Did you need something else?" she asked.

"Actually, yes. I heard you've been staying with the Seavers. Is that correct?" He shoved his glasses up his nose again and leaned a shoulder against the wall.

"Yes."

"Would you be willing to tell me where they are? I've been trying to get in touch with Cole. My godmother is his mom. She has cancer, and she really wants to see him."

Her stomach dropped.

After Harrison had run into a state trooper who had asked about the family and requested that Cole get in touch with his mother, he had tried to talk his parents into reaching out to her. Violet had joined him in the campaign, explaining how important it was for everyone to have the closure a final meeting would bring. Despite their efforts, Cole had dug in his heels and refused.

Violet didn't agree with his choice. She would have given anything to have one last conversation with either of her parents. She had told Cole that repeatedly, but he hadn't changed his mind. Despite disagreeing with his decision, Violet couldn't give away the Seavers' location. Not after everything the family had done to make certain she and Ava were safe.

"I'm sorry, I can't," she murmured.

"Can't? Or *won't*?"

"Both," she admitted. "The Seavers took me in when I had nowhere to go. They offered me a place to stay, and they didn't ask anything in return. I can't betray them by divulging where they are living."

"I understand, and I appreciate your loyalty to them, but as I explained, Bettina is really sick, and she wants to be reunited with Cole and his family before she dies." Eli rubbed the back of his neck and shifted his weight. He wasn't happy with her answer, she could see that, but he didn't argue, and he didn't try to force her into giving him the information.

"I can pass a message to Cole through Harrison. He and I have been trying to convince Cole to get in touch with his mother. It does seem like the right thing to do." Violet would be heartbroken if she reached the end of her life and had a severed relationship with Ava.

"I'd appreciate that, and I appreciate that you and Harrison have been trying. How old is he now? Seventeen? Eighteen?"

"Seventeen."

"And he likes living off the grid?"

"He is good at it," she said, hedging around the truth, because she it wasn't her place to speak for Harrison.

"Being good at something doesn't mean you enjoy it. What does he want to do with his life? You ever talk to him about it?"

"He's interested in veterinary medicine, but he's young, and that could change tomorrow."

"Sounds like he has a good head on his shoulders. I'd like to meet up with him one day. Just to get to know him. If you can pass that along, too, I'd appreciate it. He can contact me here." Eli set a business card next to the phone. "I'll grab the phone later. Just leave it on the table."

He stepped out of the room without saying goodbye, closing the door behind him.

The silence in the wake of his departure was almost deafening, the weight of his disapproval and disappointment hanging in the air. She almost followed him into the hall. Not because she planned to change her mind and give up the Seavers' location, but because she wanted to find out where Gabe was and if he was okay.

He had taken every action with her and Ava's best interest at heart, doing everything he could to make sure they got back to Anchorage safely. He had risked his life to protect theirs. She would never forget that, and she could never repay the debt. His warmth and compassion were genuine. They had nothing to do with where Violet came from or what he hoped to get from her. He cared because it was part of who he was. Deep down, where it counted most, he was a decent, upstanding, heroic human being. Being around him made her feel safe and protected, and that was something she had needed and longed for while she was living off the grid.

"We're strong, independent women, Ava, but that doesn't mean we can't appreciate and admire a man who steps in and helps us," she murmured, pulling off Ava's knit hat and kissing her downy head. Her hair was damp from sweat, the layers of bundling Violet used to keep her warm in the bunker too much for the interior of the building.

"Sorry, love," she said. "Mommy wasn't thinking. Let's get you more comfortable."

Violet took off her coat, dropping it on the back of the chair, then took Ava out of the sling. Once that was done, she unzipped the tiny snowsuit and pulled it off, smiling at her daughter.

"Is that better?" she asked, her heart filled with a terrible kind of yearning, a deep-seated need to protect the precious life God had given her.

She hadn't intended to get pregnant. She couldn't say she had been thrilled when she'd learned the news, but she had never doubted that she would love her child, and she had been wholly committed to the task of being a mother.

What she hadn't known was how quickly and deeply love happened, or how desperate she would be to make certain Ava was safe and cared for.

Violet had no family, but she knew Ariel would step in if something happened to her. She'd be the mother Ava deserved, but there was nothing official. Nothing in writing. Ariel had yet to meet the baby.

Violet picked up the phone, settling into a seat to nurse Ava. She knew she probably should call a lawyer, but the voice she really wanted to hear, the only person she really wanted to talk to, was Ariel.

She dialed the number and waited for her best friend to answer.

The team made it back to headquarters before the first flake of snow fell, but Gabe doubted they'd be there long. Paramedics had pronounced Jared Dennis dead, and the medical examiner had indicated that he had died from a gunshot wound to the head. He'd had a shallow bullet wound in his arm. One he would have easily recovered from if his best friend hadn't decided to kill him.

The cold-blooded murder shouldn't have surprised Gabe.

He had seen plenty of the uglier side of human nature.

He frowned, opening the back hatch of his SUV and letting Bear out. This was the part of the job he struggled with—doubting his decisions, worrying that he had done the wrong thing at the wrong time.

Lives depended on his ability to make good decisions under incredible pressure.

Today, he had failed.

But he had protected Violet and Ava. That had been his priority and his focus. As hard as it was to feel like he had made a mistake, he had at least done what he had set out to do.

"I hope you're not still beating yourself up about this," Hunter McCord called from across the parking lot. They had worked together for enough years to know each other well. "Will told me you were blaming your-self about what happened."

"Second-guessing my choices, maybe, but I was more worried about Violet and Ava than I was about a guy who was trying to kill us all. How are they?"

"Violet and the baby? Back at headquarters and fine, from what I've heard." Hunter opened the back of his SUV and released Juneau. The husky shook out his fur and greeted Bear with a friendly bark and play bow.

"Good. Let's make sure we keep them that way."

"You know we will."

"I'd like to have interrogated Jared. He was the weak link in their little criminal gang. If we'd apprehended him alive, he would have spilled the beans on where Lance has been hiding."

"He did," Hunter said with a quick, hard smile.

"What do you mean?"

"I just got off the phone with the ME. Jared had a wallet in his pocket. There was a key card for a motel room in it."

"What motel?" Gabe asked, ready to get back in his vehicle and head there.

Lance was an incredibly dangerous man.

He'd shot his best friend dead in front of the police.

He needed to be stopped.

"Mountain Terrace."

"The one east of Anchorage?" Gabe was familiar with the place. He'd done a few drug busts there in his younger years. A seedy motel that catered to people who didn't want to be found, it served a community that lived right on the edge of the law.

"Yes. I already called the colonel, and she's getting

us a search warrant for the motel room. Should have it in hand in the next few hours."

The founder of the K-9 team, Lorenza Gallo, had been one of the first female Alaska state troopers to work with a K-9. Ten years ago, she had put together a team of top-notch handlers and dogs to help work some of Alaska's toughest cases. Driven, high-energy, fair and to-the-point, Lorenza knew how to get things done.

"Are we planning to head over there after we question Violet?" Gabe asked. He wanted to see her, make sure she was okay and that she and her baby didn't need anything.

He also wanted to hear her side of the story.

It would be easier to ask the questions, and easier for her to answer them, when they were safe in headquarters.

Hunter's phone buzzed, and he glanced at the screen. "Ariel just texted. Violet called her. Apparently, Eli let her use a precinct phone."

"Did she say anything helpful?"

"Ariel didn't elaborate. Just said she called, sounded good and wanted her to meet the baby. Just in case."

"In case what?" They stepped into the federal building, the 1930s architecture streamlined and minimalistic. The K-9 training facility was behind the historic building, and Gabe often spent more time there than at his apartment.

"She's worried that Lance will get to her. That he'll kill her and that there won't be anyone willing to take the baby."

"Foster care is no joke. It would be better for Ava to be with someone who loves her and will be invested in her future," he said. After spending most of his childhood in foster care, shuffled from one ambivalent placement to another, he'd never felt like he belonged. And while Gabe had muddled through as best he could, he'd always longed for parents who cared about him. His mother had died when he was in elementary school, and his father had never been part of his life.

"Not that we're going to let anything happen to Violet," he added.

"Absolutely not," Hunter agreed. "Ariel is champing at the bit, wanting to see Violet and the baby, but I've asked her to stay away until we apprehend Lance. I'm concerned he'll kidnap her and use her as bait to draw Violet out."

"We're not going to let that happen, either," Gabe said. Hunter and Ariel had become close during the investigation. Now they were engaged, their lives together starting from a tragedy and turning into something wonderful.

"Back so soon, Hunter? What? Your thin blood couldn't take the cold?" Maya Rodriguez joked as she walked past with her dog, Sarge.

"You know it," he laughed as he hurried up to the stairs that led to their offices.

"How are Violet and Ava?" Gabe asked.

"Fine, but you know Violet asked for an attorney, right?" Maya said. "It might be a while before we can actually speak with her."

"Has the attorney arrived yet?" Gabe asked.

"No, but she has enough money to pay for the best, so I'd say whoever it is will be here soon with plenty of rules about what we can and can't ask and what she can and can't say." Maya sighed. "I hope she gets released soon so she can take her daughter home. The baby is adorable."

"Yes, she is," Gabe returned gruffly.

"She's in the conference room at the far end of the hall," Maya told them. "I'm going to type up some reports. If you need me, you know where to find me."

She walked off, her dog on heel beside her.

"A lawyer isn't my idea of a fun afternoon," Hunter muttered as he opened the door to the conference room and stepped inside.

Gabe followed.

Violet was seated at a table, muted sunlight streaming in through the windows and highlighting the pale gold strands of her hair. The makeup she'd been wearing had worn off, and her skin was alabaster with a few freckles on her nose and cheeks. He'd studied photos of her during the months she'd been hiding, and he had never noticed them.

She smiled as she met his eyes, the kind of welcoming smile that passed between friends. They had spent a long night in a cabin in the woods, cut off from the world and waiting for trouble to find them. Maybe that had created a bond between them. Whatever the case, his heart responded, his pulse ratcheting up as he looked into her eyes.

"Ms. James," Hunter began, taking a seat across the table from her. "I hear you've requested an attorney. Any idea when your counsel will arrive?"

"I've changed my mind and am going to waive my right to an attorney. I haven't done anything wrong, and I don't have anything to hide," she responded.

"Mind if we get that on tape?" Hunter asked, pulling out a small recording device and setting it on the table.

"Not at all."

He began the recording, and she repeated her statement, Ava cradled in her arms, tiny fingers curled into fists, cheeks pink. A fragile life that Gabe felt fiercely protective of.

He didn't like seeing kids hurt.

It bothered him to hear them crying.

In a perfect world, no child would ever be homeless, loveless or neglected. It wasn't a perfect world, but he had striven to do his part to help kids in the community. Gabe ran the rec program at his church, supervising after-school basketball and football games and offering plenty of activities for at-risk youth. He also volunteered at a local shelter, mentoring young men looking to make better choices in their lives.

His protective nature ran deep, but what he felt for Violet and Ava surprised him. It felt personal, as if they were more than just another mother and child who needed help. As if they were somehow connected more deeply than that.

He'd never thought about what it would be like to have a family of his own. He'd only known that if he did, he would do everything possible to make certain they felt safe and loved.

But Ava wasn't his child. And Violet wasn't his wife. He had no reason to feel such a deep tug of protectiveness toward them, but he couldn't deny it, and when the baby started fussing during the interview, he offered to walk her around the room to calm her.

Violet placed her in his arms, and he held her close, gently patting her back. It still felt awkward and unnatural. His years of not being around infants hadn't prepared him for comforting a fussy, tired newborn, but holding Ava felt…right and good. He met Violet's eyes, and she smiled gently, her expression tender. His heart swelled with the need to keep her and her baby safe, to stand beside her and do everything he could to make sure they had what they needed to thrive.

The feeling took him by surprise.

He considered himself a hard-hitting, tough cop who had been through enough in life to not be swayed by emotion. He was a pragmatist with just enough cynicism to keep himself from falling for every sob story he heard during interviews with suspects. He didn't expect or want to be drawn to someone the way he felt drawn to Violet, but he couldn't deny that he felt something compelling when he looked into her eyes.

He walked to the window, looking out into the fading day.

The sun was being swallowed by dark clouds, the few flakes of snow that had been falling suddenly turning to sheets of ice and rain. Not good weather to be out in. Maybe that would drive Lance back to the motel. Troopers had already been dispatched there and were sitting in unmarked cars, waiting for his return.

If he tried to set foot there, Lance would be stopped. Until then, Gabe was going to stick close to Violet and Ava. He might not be an expert at taking care of newborns, but he knew how to protect the people he cared about. Right now, they were at the top of his list of priorities. He had found them in the cabin in the woods, and it was his responsibility to make certain that didn't cost either of them their lives.

NINE

Violet answered every questioned she was asked.

Some of them she answered two or three times.

Trooper McCord finally finished the interview, hit the stop button on the small recording device that sat on the table and leaned back in his chair. "We appreciate your cooperation, Ms. James. You and your baby have been through a lot. It wasn't my intention to make it worse. I hope that you understand, we're just trying to get to the bottom of what happened."

"I do," she assured him, glancing at Gabe, wondering if he planned on questioning her, too.

Up until now, he'd been mostly quiet, pacing the width of the room with Ava in his arms, his hair blueblack in the overhead light.

He met her eyes and offered a reassuring smile.

She should have felt nothing. No tiny little thrill of attraction. No acknowledgment that Gabe was very handsome, very charming and very heroic. But apparently her heart had other ideas.

"I can take her now," she murmured, her pulse thumping wildly in her chest. This was what the beginning of love felt like. She didn't know how she knew it, but she did. What she'd felt before was nothing compared to the deep, soul-stirring need she felt when Gabe was around.

Don't go there, she warned herself sternly, Whatever she might be feeling was pointless. She'd been there and done that. Looked into the eyes of a handsome and charming man. Believed his smile and his lies. She'd paid for that in ways that had permanently changed her.

There was no going back, no trusting blindly. She was wiser. Smarter. More confident of herself and her place in the world. She didn't need a man to validate her worth, and she certainly didn't need one for financial support. Living with the Seavers had taught her how easily she could adapt to different places and different circumstances. It had also taught her how to be content with herself. At night, when the Seavers went to their small rooms and she lay on the cot in the living area, she'd had no one to talk to. Just her thoughts and her prayers.

It had been enough.

It would continue to be enough.

But she still felt her heart melt as Gabe walked toward her.

"She's out cold," he said softly, handing her the baby, his fingers brushing her knuckles. Warmth spread up her arm, and her cheeks heated.

He had a way about him. A confidence that was more appealing than she wanted it to be.

"Thanks," she murmured, placing Ava in the baby carrier and standing.

She moved a few feet away, shoving her arms into

her coat, ready to leave. But, of course, she had no car and no money.

Aside from the borrowed phone that still lay on the table, she had nothing but the clothes on her back and the few things in her pack. "If we're done here, I'd like to go home. I'll need to call an Uber," she said.

"You're really planning to return to your home?" Gabe asked.

"Yes. There's another storm blowing in, and I'll feel better having Ava in a safe place," she replied.

"I'm not sure your house is the safest place for the two of you." He frowned, his attention shifting to Trooper McCord. "What about the safe house outside town? Is it available?"

"Should be. I'll give Lorenza a call. If she approves it, we can head over there now. Then go to the motel."

"Motel?" Violet asked, her head pounding with fatigue and hunger. She'd barely slept the previous night, and she hadn't eaten since the evening before. Nursing a baby and hiking through the snow burned calories that she didn't have to spare.

"Lance and Jared were holed up in one. We found the key card in Jared's wallet," Gabe explained.

"Did Jared…survive?" she asked, knowing that he hadn't but wishing she were wrong. So many horrible things had happened because of choices she had made. If she'd broken up with Lance the first time she had wondered about his intentions, two people might still be alive and Ariel never would have been hurt.

"I'm afraid not," Gabe said gently.

"Did Lance shoot him?"

"Yes."

"They were friends for most of their lives," she whispered, trying to wrap her mind around the fact that a man she had thought she loved had killed two people in cold blood. One of them his best friend.

"People like Lance don't care about friendship. They care about getting what they want. Jared had an injury to his arm. Lance probably thought he was going to be a liability. Rather than leave him behind and risk him becoming a witness for the state, he killed him." Trooper McCord was matter-of-fact, his expression hard, his gaze sharp. "If you think he won't do the same to you, you're mistaken."

"I'm not that much of a fool."

"You aren't a fool, Violet," Gabe cut in. "Lance is an exceptional liar and manipulator. He had us conned until we got a good look at the evidence."

"I still feel responsible for what happened to Cal and to Jared."

"The responsibility for their deaths rests on Lance's shoulders, not yours," Gabe said. "He committed the crimes, and he is the one who is going to pay. But he's dangerous and unpredictable. Until we have him in custody, the best thing you can do is allow us to offer the protection you and your daughter need."

Gabe was right… Violet knew it. A safe house would keep her hidden until Lance was behind bars, but she was desperate to go home. Just for a few minutes. Just to check on the property, to see it through fresh eyes, to grab a few things that would remind her of her parents and the happy life they'd had together. "If I agree to go to the safe house, will you let me stop by my place first?

I've been away for seven months, and I'm feel like I've forgotten what it's like to be home." Her voice broke, and to her horror, tears welled in her eyes.

She'd never been much of a crier.

There were better ways to deal with emotions.

She turned away from Gabe and Trooper McCord, walking to the windows and staring out into the fading day.

A few moments later, she heard the door open and close. But she didn't look to see who had come or gone. She didn't want anyone to see the tears that were sliding down her cheeks. Still, voices carried through the door. A discussion between Gabe and Trooper McCord, she thought, but she didn't get closer to the door to try to hear what they were saying. For the past few months, it had seemed as if her life was out of her control. She'd had no choice in how or where she lived, because she'd had to stay hidden. She'd hoped that returning to Anchorage would change that.

The door opened and closed again.

Violet wiped the moisture from her cheeks, hoping she didn't look as dejected and defeated as she felt. She'd fought so hard for so long to keep moving forward and believing that one day things would go back to normal.

But how could things ever be normal if Lance was on the loose?

"Violet?" Gabe touched her shoulder. "It's going to be okay."

"You can't know that, and neither can I."

"Maybe not, but I can do everything in my power to keep you and Ava safe."

"Why?" She turned to face him.

"Because I'm a police officer. My job is to protect and serve."

"I don't want anyone else hurt because of the choices I made." Lance had done enough damage, and she was terrified of what he might do next. Would he go after her friends? Her coworkers?

Would he try to harm Ava?

The thought made her cold with dread.

"We're going to do everything possible to bring him into custody quickly. Until we do, the safe house is your best option. I spoke with Hunter. We can bring you to your place before we go there. You can pack a few things for yourself and Ava."

"I appreciate that," she said, her throat tight with more tears. But she didn't let them fall. She needed to focus on gathering the things she'd missed most from home—photos of her parents. Her mother's worn Bible. The quilt her grandmother had made.

She'd lived a life of privilege. She'd always known that. Her parents had instilled a sense of grateful acknowledgment. They'd taught her to be generous with what she had, to appreciate it and to understand how fortunate she was. She had always valued the house, the heat, the food, but she had overlooked the smaller things—the trinkets, the keepsakes, the items that had no intrinsic value but were rich in memories.

Those were the things she had missed most when she was in the bunker.

"You ready to head out, Gabe?" Maya Rodriguez walked into the room, her Malinois at her side. "Sean and Grace are already in his vehicle."

"Are you ready?" Gabe asked Violet.

She nodded. Scared. Excited. Ready to return home. Even if it was just for a few minutes.

"Let's head out." Gabe took her arm, his fingers curved around her bicep. The gentle touch reminded her of all the things she'd never had with Lance. He had never made her feel safe, and she had never really felt she could count on him.

He'd been attentive, showering her with words of praise, with gifts, with dinner dates and flowers. She'd been so desperate for love that she had convinced herself that those things were true signs of commitment.

But Gabe's hand on her arm? That felt more real than anything Lance had done.

She didn't allow herself to dwell on that as she stepped outside and got in Gabe's vehicle. She had more important things to worry about.

Lance was still on the loose.

No matter how determined Gabe was to protect her, the threat was real, and she would be foolish to ignore it. She'd go inside the house, gather the things she wanted, and then she'd allow herself to be taken to the safe house. As much as she hated the idea, she'd stay there until Lance was apprehended.

That was the smart thing to do.

Not just for herself, but for her daughter.

And right now, Ava's well-being was the most important thing in the world to her.

Violet's house sat in the middle of ten acres overlooking Campbell Lake. The impressive facade hid an equally impressive interior. Hardwood floors. Plush throw rugs. Huge fireplaces.

Gabe took in the details as he followed Violet up a curved staircase and into a large bedroom suite. He thought she'd grab clothes and toiletries. Maybe a laptop or electronic gadget of some sort.

Instead, she put several photos into a small suitcase. Then she walked into an adjoining room, and he stood on the threshold as she took folded baby clothes from a tall dresser.

"I bought a few things when I found out I was pregnant," she said as if she needed to explain herself.

"There's nothing wrong with that," he responded, walking to a window that overlooked the front yard. Maya and Sean were in their vehicles, keeping their eyes out for trouble.

"No. There isn't, but I was buying things and hiding them from Lance. I didn't want to tell him about the baby. I was afraid of what his reaction would be."

"I'm sorry," he said, turning to face her again. "No woman should ever have to feel that way."

She looked tired, sad and very, very beautiful.

He wanted to tell her that.

Tell her just how lovely she was. Just how deserving she was of all the things that every person should have—acceptance, friendship, admiration and kindness.

"Don't be. I made my choices, and I got the consequences of them. I have no one to blame but myself for how things played out." She tossed a pack of disposable diapers in the suitcase. "I almost called off the wedding the day before we went on our wilderness tour. If I had, none of this would have happened. Lives would have been saved. No one would have been hurt."

"We've been down this road before, and you know

what I'm going to say—you can't blame yourself for Lance's actions."

"And you know what I'm going to say," she responded with a tired smile. "I can blame myself for being an idiot. My parents raised me to be smarter than this." She dragged the suitcase into the hall and walked into a large office. A mahogany desk sat in the center of the room, facing windows that looked across the lake.

Violet took a photo from the desk and tucked it into the suitcase, then opened a drawer and pulled out a well-worn leather Bible. "My mother's," she explained. "She read it every morning and evening. She'd be disappointed if she knew some of the choices I've made."

"Or, maybe, she'd be proud that you've persisted and overcome enormous adversity," he suggested, not wanting her to cry again. He'd seen the tears on her cheeks at headquarters, and it had taken all he had not to brush them away, pull her into his arms and promise that everything would be okay.

She walked to an oil painting and pulled it off the wall, revealing a wall safe. "Maybe," she said with a half smile. "My mom and dad were always accepting of others, and they didn't hold things against people, so I guess she wouldn't hold my poor choices against me."

"Sounds like your parents were exceptional people."

"They were." She unlocked the safe and took out a stack of bills. "This is legal, by the way. No ill-gotten gains in the safe. My father always insisted on keeping enough cash at the house to pay bills for a month."

"Obviously, your father's bills are way higher than mine," he joked as she put the cash in her suitcase.

"Probably higher than most. He liked to help people,

and he never turned someone away if they needed it. I usually just leave the cash in the safe, but my wallet was at the cabin the day of our wilderness excursion. I don't have access to my bank cards, and I'd really like to buy Ava a crib. She deserves a comfortable place to sleep." She kissed the top of her daughter's downy head.

"I'm not sure shopping is the best idea right now." Not with Lance still on the loose.

"I wasn't planning on making the purchase myself. I was hoping someone could give the cash to Ariel Potter. She could buy it for me."

"We'll make sure Ava has a crib," he said, sidestepping the request to get Ariel involved. She hadn't seen who pushed her off the cliff, but the renowned husky trainer hadn't wavered in her belief that Violet was innocent of any crimes. Her insistence that the team focus in other directions had been part of the reason why Lance and Jared had become suspects so quickly.

"I know it probably seems like a silly thing. She can sleep with me, and that will be fine, too, but the day she was born, I felt like such a horrible mother. I had nothing for her. Just some clothes Harrison bought at the thrift store and some makeshift diapers."

"You said she came early," he commented, wishing she wasn't berating herself over something she'd had no control over.

"I'd had eight and a half months to prepare, and I'd done nothing. I guess I kept hoping things would change and I'd be able to return home before she arrived. I should have pulled my head out of the sand months before I went into labor. The Seavers tried to get me focused on getting ready for her arrival, but I kept putting it off."

"You were dealing with a lot, Violet. Don't beat yourself up over it."

"She deserves better," she replied, her voice breaking, a tear trickling down her cheek.

"What is better than love?" he asked, nudging her chin up so that she met his eyes. "What is better than giving your child every bit of your heart?"

"A home with four walls and some windows. A real floor. Light streaming in," she responded, not stepping away from his touch. Instead she just stood there, looking into his eyes and studying his face, searching for something.

Maybe honesty. Integrity. Honor.

"Those are things, Violet. I had them when I was a kid. Walls. Windows. Light. Yards to play in. But after my mother died, I didn't have love. I'd have traded it all for that."

"Gabe, I'm so sorry," she said, another tear slipping down her cheek. Only this time, he thought she might be crying for him. For the confused kid he'd been, shuffled from home to home, uncaring placement to uncaring placement.

"Hey, it's okay. I grew up, and I used what I learned from my time in foster care to help me do better for kids in Anchorage. I've been a big brother for years, and I'm involved in foster education and training," he responded, brushing the tear away and giving her and Ava a gentle hug.

It wasn't meant to be more than that.

Just a quick and easy expression of friendship, understanding and comfort, but she fit perfectly in his arms, her hands fluttering near his ribs for a moment before settling on his waist, her forehead resting on his chest. Ava was between them, her small body sheltered by two people who would do anything to protect her.

Gabe felt it all deeply.

The two vulnerable lives he was holding close.

The vastness of the wilderness they'd survived.

The danger that lurked just beyond the walls of the house Violet had spent her childhood in.

He brushed her hair back, the thick strands falling past her shoulder. Flax and honey. Burnished by days spent outdoors. "Don't cry," he rasped.

"I'm sorry," she repeated, finally stepping back, her cheeks pink, freckles dancing across her nose.

With distance between them, he could think again.

Bear was near a window, staring out into the dusky light. Icy rain was falling in sheets, mixing with flakes of snow and pea-size pieces of hail. Lance had proven that he wasn't averse to bad weather. He hadn't returned to the motel.

He could be anywhere. And Gabe would be smart to keep that in mind. He needed keep his thoughts and his attention on the case. Getting too deeply involved could only cause problems.

He watched as Violet walked to the dresser, opening drawers and grabbing clothes. She didn't seem to notice or care what color or what item she was taking. Rather, she just shoved everything in the suitcase, added a brush and toothbrush from the bathroom, and then hastily zipped it closed.

"Everything okay?" he asked.

"Yeah." She sighed. "I was just hoping to spend the night here."

"I wish we could allow that, but it's not safe. It won't be until Lance is behind bars." He grabbed the suitcase and called to Bear.

"I know." She sounded tired.

She *looked* tired. There were dark circles under her eyes, her shoulders were bowed and he could see the vertebrae in her neck, each one clearly delineated.

Gabe recalled that they hadn't eaten since the previous night, and she was a nursing mother. That concerned him.

Her gauntness concerned him.

And her pale skin and the shakiness of her hand as she set the security code and stepped outside made him wonder if he should be taking her to the hospital rather than a safe house.

"Maybe we should get you checked out by a doctor," he suggested as she closed the door and used a code to lock it.

"I was at the doctor yesterday morning. Well, the midwife. But she gave me a physical and a clean bill of health."

"Really?" he asked, waving to Maya, who had jumped out of her car and was hurrying toward them.

"She wants me to eat more, but other than that, I'm in good shape."

"We'll make sure the safe house has a fully stocked pantry," he promised.

"Some extra diapers would be nice, too," she responded.

"We'll make sure you have those as well." He opened the passenger door and waited while she climbed in.

He needed to buy an infant car seat. Violet hadn't mentioned it, but he put it on his mental list. Safety was paramount. Even in situations like these.

"Gabe!" Maya called. "Can I talk to you for a second?"

"Sure." He closed the door and joined her. Bear lumbered beside him, happy to be outdoors, the rain and sleet bouncing off his thick coat.

"What's up?" he asked, surveying the area while he spoke, looking for any sign that Lance was nearby.

"We got the search warrant for the motel, and patrol officers have already made entry. Lance isn't there."

"Did we expect him to be?"

"No, but there's plenty of evidence that he was. Clothes. Shoes. A watch with his name engraved on the back. They also found a couple of plane tickets as well as fake IDs for Lance and Jared. Passports. Driver's licenses. Everything they needed to leave the country without being detected."

"So, why didn't they?" he wondered aloud, brushing icy rain from his cheek.

"Interesting question, and I think we have an answer. The tickets were dated for the day after the wilderness tour began. Looks like Lance and his buddy planned to skip out, get on a plane and leave the country."

"A runaway groom?"

"That would be my guess. When we subpoenaed his financials, Violet and Lance had a joint account. Remember? Approximately two million dollars transferred in to open it. Then all but a couple of grand transferred back out the night before the excursion?"

"I remember," he said, glancing at his car, wondering if Violet had any idea that Lance had planned to leave before he'd married her. Gabe had spent hours interviewing her friends and the people she worked for. According to them, she was intelligent, hardworking and compassionate. She didn't get duped in business and ran the family oil company with the same efficiency and focus as her father.

How had someone like that ended up with someone like Lance?

No doubt the guy was a chameleon, changing colors to match his environment. People who knew him through his business called him a shark. Old friends hadn't had very flattering things to say. New ones loved him, praised him and thought he could do no wrong.

Even his family was at odds when it came to Lance. His parents thought he was a perfect son with perfect manners who lived a nearly perfect life. But his sister called him a liar and a manipulator. Gabe thought her opinion was closest to the truth.

"You feel sorry for her," Maya said.

"She didn't ask for this. She went into the relationship believing Lance was everything he claimed to be."

"She's fortunate she's alive to talk about it. We'd better head out. The storm is going to come in hard in the next few hours. The safe house is nice, but it's out in the middle of nowhere on that back road. Not easy to get to when the ice gets thick."

"Did Lorenza approve officers to stay at the house

with Violet?" he asked, scanning the yard, the lake, the shrubs that lined the driveway.

"Yeah. You probably have the text."

"Want to give me a recap?" he replied, still scanning their surroundings. The dogs seemed relaxed, but something felt off. He couldn't put his finger on what, and he couldn't see anything alarming.

"She has a few of us running shifts, but you're scheduled to do the overnights. I let her know that I'd be happy to switch out with you."

"I'm currently the one with the freest social schedule, so that makes sense," Gabe said. In the past year, most of the members of the team had fallen in love and gotten engaged or married. They were just as committed to their jobs, but they also had other priorities. People who loved them. Families that needed them.

Gabe was still a bachelor, living in a one-bedroom apartment. That was what he'd wanted. It was how he had always planned to live. He'd done his time on the dating circuit when he was younger and had even been engaged at one time. But his long hours and commitment to work had created tension with his ex-fiancée. Destiny had wanted time and attention that he hadn't been able to give.

Or, maybe, he hadn't wanted to.

The day she'd tossed the engagement ring in his face and told him she was done, he had been more relieved than heartbroken. That had made him wonder if he was like his father—a man who had walked away from his wife and child without a backward glance. Gabe had no memories of him, and he had very few of his mother.

He had no idea how to parent or how to create the kind of happy family he had longed for when he was a child.

He hadn't thought he wanted to learn, but meeting Violet had changed that. Watching her with Ava had made him long to be part of something bigger than his job, bigger than his career. He wanted to go home to people who were waiting with open arms and open hearts.

"Like I said, I can switch out with you. When David was the security chief for the cruise line, he worked all kinds of odd shifts, so he totally gets what it's like not to have a nine-to-five job. Plus, he isn't the type of guy who would give me a hard time about my schedule, anyway. If he was, I wouldn't be with him."

Maya had met David Garrison while working undercover on a cruise ship, and the two had been inseparable since. Gabe couldn't deny the affection and love he had seen between them.

"I appreciate it, but I'll be fine." He opened the back of the SUV and called for Bear to get in. The temperature was dropping, hail falling in sheets and bouncing off the ground. Ava fussed, a quiet mewl that reminded him of a kitten.

He needed to get them to safety.

The nagging feeling of danger wouldn't leave, and he had learned to always trust his gut.

"Let's head out," he said, closing the hatch and rounding the side of his vehicle.

Maya hurried to her SUV and hopped in.

The community was posh, the properties spread out and sitting on several acres each. Most of them gated. The long driveway that led back to the road was lined with lights. Even so, visibility was low, the evening dusky and gray. The gate into the property was open. Just as it had been when they'd arrived. Nothing looked out of place or seemed amiss. But Gabe was tense and on edge just the same. He was certain trouble was coming.

Maya drove through the gate first. Sean followed. Gabe was next, cruising toward the gate at slow speed, that odd disquiet still lodged in his chest. The gate swung shut, blocking their exit and preventing anyone's entrance in.

"It doesn't close on its own," Violet said. "It stays open unless you punch the code in from the house to close it or use the remote I have in my car."

"Is there a keypad on the gate?" Gabe asked.

"Yes, but you have to get out to punch it in, and I don't think that's a good idea." Her voice was shaking, and she'd shifted in her seat to look toward the house.

He was on the radio, calling for immediate backup, when she grabbed his arm. "I think I see flames."

"Where?"

"The house is on fire!" she shouted, opening the door.

The first bullet hit the window, pinging off bulletproof glass. He had the door closed before the second hit. "Stay down, Violet!"

He glanced at Ava, felt his heart shudder with fear and the desperate need to protect them both.

Bear barked, the frantic warning coming seconds before a barrage of bullets hit the front of the SUV.

Gabe was on the radio, shouting information above the chaos. Maya's vehicle was outside the gate, Sean's parked beside it. Both of them were taking cover behind open doors as they tried to get a clear shot, but the evening had gone quiet again, the barrage of bullets ending as quickly as it had begun.

Lance would be a fool to stay nearby.

He'd taken his shots. He'd tried to get Violet out of the vehicle. He'd failed.

He'd be on the run.

And he was about to have three K-9 officers chasing him down.

"What's the gate code?" Gabe asked after helping Violet back into her seat.

She gave it.

"Stay here."

He jumped out of the SUV, opened the back hatch to free Bear and locked the doors. A patrol car pulled up outside the gate as he entered the code. When the gate swung open, the officers raced inside. Gabe couldn't resist looking back at Violet and Ava before following suit. He reminded himself that they were safe as long as they remained in the vehicle.

Plus, he had a murderer to chase down.

But for the first time in his career, he felt hesitant to go on the hunt. Not because he was afraid of finding the perp, but because he was worried about what he was leaving behind.

A vulnerable woman and newborn.

Two innocent people who had done nothing to deserve the trouble they'd found themselves in.

He wanted to make that right.

He needed to.

He called to Bear, radioed his location and headed away from the lights and sirens.

TEN

The fire was minor.

Just a pile of debris lit with accelerant near the front corner of the house. No damage to the facade. Just a few smudges of soot on the fieldstone used for the foundation.

Violet had been shown the photos, but she hadn't been allowed to go back to the house. A K-9 trooper had ushered her and Ava into a waiting vehicle and driven them away.

They'd wound through Anchorage, taking back roads and main roads. She knew the area well, and she tracked their progress. They were going in circles, revisiting routes. She assumed the trooper was making certain they weren't being followed.

Ava whimpered from the infant car seat the trooper had provided.

She was hungry. They were way past feeding time. She probably needed to be changed.

"It's okay, sweetheart. We'll be there soon," she cooed.

"Won't we?" she added, directing the question at the auburn-haired officer who was escorting her to the safe house. The giant dog lying in the back lifted its head and sniffed the air.

"Yes," the trooper said. "Sorry this is taking a while. We want to make certain Lance can't follow us to the safe house. I'm Trooper Poppy Walsh, by the way. Should have introduced myself earlier, but I had orders to get you out fast. My dog, Stormy, will let us know if there's anything to worry about once we arrive at our destination. She goes after poachers and is good at detecting people who are lurking where they shouldn't be."

"I appreciate the effort you're putting into keeping me and Ava safe," Violet said. "I'm sorry that I caused so much trouble."

"Honey, you didn't cause a thing. Lance Wells did. But we'll find him, and we'll put him in prison. Then your life can go back to normal."

Normal?

Violet wasn't sure she knew what that was. Not anymore. She'd had normal with her parents, and after they'd died, she'd thought she'd found it again with Lance. That had been a charade.

When she returned to her old life, what would it be?

Living with the Seavers had made her realize how little she had been doing for herself. Sure, she washed her own clothes, made her own meals and drove where she needed to go. Her parents had taught her to be self-sufficient, but she had never had to worry about where a meal would come from. She certainly hadn't had to tend a fire through the night to keep warm.

That said, she'd tried to give back before she'd gone on the run.

She'd contributed to the community. Had given to

charity. She'd even volunteered in soup kitchens and women's shelters. Violet had always had compassion for the people she was serving, but she had never really been able to empathize, because she'd had no idea what it felt like to rely on the charity of others.

Now she knew.

She understood how tenuous an existence that was. How humbling and how hard to have to ask for help and pray you would receive it.

The Seavers' kindness had kept her fed, clothed and warm for seven months. The medical clinic had offered free pregnancy care without asking for anything in return.

She would never forget that.

Her view of the world, of life and of her place in it had changed, and she needed to change with it.

Violet didn't just want to return to her old life. She wanted to return to her community. Be better. More committed to making a difference.

She planned to start with the medical clinic. It was run on a shoestring budget by doctors, nurses and midwives who volunteered their time to help pregnant women.

Once this nightmare with Lance finally ended, she would volunteer her time and experience to help expand the clinic's service to the community. She had the resources, and thanks to her father's tutorage, she had the business know-how.

"You doing okay?" Poppy asked, breaking the silence.

"I'm fine. Just anxious to get to the other side of all this."

"You've been running from Lance for a long time. It seems like a little peace is past due," Poppy said kindly.

"I just hope Lance doesn't hurt anyone else. He's already done enough damage."

"We're doing everything we can to keep that from happening." The SUV left the main road, the pouring sleet and hail pinging off the windshield. The road might have been gravel or dirt. Violet couldn't tell. She could barely see the trees that crowded to either side.

It was dangerous weather to be out in.

Especially dangerous for someone hunting a killer.

She had been trying not to think about Gabe and Bear, out in the dark and the cold, going after a man who wouldn't hesitate to kill them, but her thoughts circled back to them again and again.

They were risking their lives for hers.

She couldn't forget that.

Gabe had said his job was to protect and serve. She got that. But when push came to shove, most people looked out for themselves first and worried about everyone else later. That was a lesson being involved in a multibillion-dollar corporation had taught her. It was what having wealth had taught her. Her parents had been kindhearted and compassionate, but they had raised Violet to understand that people would take advantage if they could. It still shocked her that she had fallen for Lance…that she had set herself up to be victimized, and she hadn't even realized she was doing it.

Never again.

She could do life on her own, and she would.

But she couldn't deny Gabe's integrity, his honor and his commitment to his job. He had proven himself again and again, protecting her and Ava when he could have simply protected himself.

Poppy pulled up in front of a log cabin–style home, parking under a portico that sat near a detached three-car garage.

"This is the safe house?" Violet asked, surprised by how nice it was.

She wasn't sure what she'd been expecting. Maybe a small hunting cabin out in the wilderness?

"Yes. It belonged to a senator who left it to the state when he passed away. We have a few properties like this. They stay in the family's name, but we pay the taxes and upkeep. That makes it difficult for criminals to identify them as safe houses."

Poppy got out of the SUV, released her dog and helped Violet unlatch the infant car seat.

They walked inside together, entering a foyer that opened into a hearth room. A fireplace was central to the design, old river stones gleaming in dimmed chandelier light.

"Your bedroom is the first one to the right upstairs. I'm going to get a fire started. You go make yourself and your daughter comfortable. Doesn't look like you brought anything with you?"

"I had a suitcase in Gabe's car," she responded.

"He'll be here shortly. So you'll have all of it then. In the meantime, we were able to get a crib and some baby stuff. It's all in the room."

"That was fast."

"We have been chasing Lance for seven months, so from our perspective things are going slowly." Poppy walked to the fireplace and tossed kindling in. The trooper seemed done talking, and Violet was tired, her head pounding, her body leaden.

She headed up the curved staircase and onto a wide landing that served as an office area. Her room was the only one with an open door. She walked in, her heart stuttering when she saw the white crib set up against one wall.

Whoever had purchased it had also bought a changing table.

There was a rocking chair in the corner with a few throw pillows tossed on the wooden seat. A twin bed stood against another wall. Two doors flanked a tall dresser. One led to a bathroom. The other led to a closet.

Violet took Ava from the car seat and changed her, humming softly as the baby fussed. It had been a long day. It wasn't surprising that the newborn was disgruntled.

"It's almost time to eat," she said, wrapping Ava in a blanket she found in the changing table. There were packages of onesies, a few sleepers and bibs.

Someone had thought of everything, and that kindness made Violet's eyes well with tears.

"We are going to repay all of them, sweetheart," she murmured as she sat in the rocking chair and began to nurse.

The house was quiet. Nothing but the soft sound of sleet hitting the roof drifted into the room. Heat poured from a vent in the floor, warming Violet's cold toes.

This was what she had imagined the beginning of motherhood would be like.

Peaceful.

Secure.

Filled with warmth and love.

Please, God, help me provide those things for my daughter, she prayed, wishing she had the Bible she'd packed.

She was too tired to read, but it would be nice to hold it, to feel the leather cover worn smooth from her mother's hands. To know how often her parents had read it together, praying over each other and over her.

Violet had wanted that for her daughter.

She had been willing to compromise, to go through with a wedding that had begun to feel like a mistake in order to give her a family, but that had been a foolish mistake. Even if she had married Lance, it never would have worked out. He wasn't the kind of man Gabe was. He didn't have the same set of values.

Gabe.

She couldn't stop thinking about him.

He had been there for her when no one else could be. She would never forget that, and she would never forget him, or the way she felt when she looked into his eyes. Ava finished eating, and she patted her back gently, rocking to a tune playing in her head. Some old song her parents used to dance to.

She missed them. Missed the life they'd had. But she could create something special for Ava. She could make it a good life. Even without family connections.

Stormy barked, the scrabble of her feet on hardwood floor drifting into the room. No panic, though. No shouted warnings from Poppy. Just the quiet murmur of voices that let Violet know more troopers had arrived.

Had Gabe?

Her heart skipped a beat at the notion of seeing his

handsome face again. Despite everything, she wanted to gaze into his kind blue eyes. Hear his deep, comforting voice. Because when she was in his presence, she felt safe. Cared for. A little less alone. And beyond that, she was worried about him, terrified that he would have a fatal run-in with Lance. He and Bear weren't the targets, but Lance had shown that he would kill anyone who got in the way of what he wanted.

He wanted the money.

Two million dollars that he probably would have transferred to a personal account and left town with, if she had given him the opportunity.

If she gave it to him now, would he leave town?

Leave *her* alone?

Let her raise Ava in peace?

She couldn't predict what he would do, but if she had a phone, she could access her accounts and let him have what he wanted. Anything to see an end to this nightmare.

She crossed the room and put Ava in the crib.

A real mattress. Real sheets.

Those things seemed so precious now.

"Sleep well, sweet one," she whispered, kissing the baby's cheek. Then she turned on a bedside lamp, turned off the overhead light and walked out of the room.

The office area was set up with a desk and a computer. She pulled out the chair and took a seat.

"Planning to do some work?"

She whirled around, met Gabe's eyes.

His hair was wet from melting sleet, his jaw shadowed by the beginning of a beard. He had her suitcase in one hand and Bear's lead in the other, and he looked better than any man who had been out in the elements for a couple hours should.

"I was hoping to use the computer," she said, trying to ignore the way her pulse jumped and her stomach flipped when she looked into his eyes.

"For?"

"Online banking," she admitted.

"The cash you brought isn't enough?" He frowned.

"I was thinking about transferring money to the account I opened with Lance."

"Why?" His expression was cold, hard and unreadable. Whatever he thought about her idea, he was keeping to himself until he had more information.

"Because it's what he wants. It's all he wants. He can take it and go to Bangkok, or wherever else he might like to live."

"He's a criminal, Violet. He'll be a fugitive. You'll be aiding and abetting."

She hadn't thought about that.

Sighing, she glanced at the room where Ava was sleeping.

So many people had already been hurt. Two people had died. Ariel had nearly lost her life. All over money.

"How long would I be in jail?" she asked.

"You aren't serious?" He scowled, putting the suitcase down and motioning for Bear to sit.

"I can't risk anyone else being hurt, Gabe. Not if I can stop it."

"Violet, you *can't* stop it. That's what I need you to understand." He crouched in front of her, holding both her hands, his palms warm against her cold skin. "He'll

take the money, and he'll still come after you. If not because he wants revenge, then because he thinks he can
get more financial reward."

"I won't give him more," she argued. "Just the
amount he thought he was going to have."

But deep down she knew she wasn't being rational.
Desperation and fatigue weren't a good combination. "I
can see that you know I'm right," he said, staring into
her eyes, studying her face, looking at her the way no
one ever had. As if he wanted to know everything. All
the easy things and the hard ones.

"Maybe." She shifted her gaze, uncomfortable with
how much he could see. How easily the truth was reflected in her face and eyes.

"I have something for you, but I don't want to give
it to you if you're going to use it to transfer the money
into that account."

"What?" she asked, looking into his eyes again.

Her breath caught. Her thoughts fled.

He was close enough that she could see the fine lines
near the corners of his eyes, a small scar just below his
left ear. Specks of brown in his dark blue eyes.

"Your phone. We'd collected it as evidence. Eli, our
tech guy, got it working and put in a new SIM card to
make certain Lance couldn't track it. We don't need it
any longer, and I got permission to return it to you. I
thought you could call your friends and employees. Let
them know that you're okay." He took it from his pocket
and set it in her hand.

"You're not going to make me vow not to transfer
the funds before you let me have it?" she asked, deeply
touched by the gesture.

"I trust you to make the best decision, Violet. You're an intelligent and savvy woman. You know what's best."

He was right.

She did.

As much as she hated to admit it.

And no matter what it cost her, she knew she couldn't give Lance what he wanted to accomplish her goals.

"Thank you," she said, leaning forward and kissing his cheek.

A quick gesture of friendship that she had exchanged with dozens of people over the years.

Only he wasn't other people.

Heat spread across her cheeks, and she jumped up.

Too quickly.

The world spun. The phone dropped from her hand. Gabe said something she couldn't quite hear.

And then she was falling, body numb, unable to fight whatever was pulling her down.

Gabe caught Violet before she hit the floor, scooping her into his arms and shouting for Poppy before carrying her into her room.

A single lamp glowed on a small table near the bed.

He laid Violet on top of the blanket.

"Violet? Can you hear me?" he said, his pulse racing, adrenaline rushing through him as he touched the pulse-point in her neck.

Poppy rushed into the room, her eyes wide with surprise and worry.

"What happened?" she asked.

"She passed out."

"She's a new mom. That could mean a lot of different things. We need to call an ambulance and get her to the hospital."

"No. I'm fine," Violet murmured, opening her eyes and struggling up onto her elbows. "I don't need to go to the hospital."

"You passed out. You *aren't* fine," Gabe growled, relieved that she'd regained consciousness but also incredibly frustrated that he couldn't do more for her. That he couldn't snap his fingers and make her world right. That he couldn't change what had happened and give her back her life.

She had been so thankful for the phone. Legitimately grateful in such a profound way that his heart had ached for her. Seven months with no contact with friends, family and coworkers was a long time. Being pregnant, living out in the wilderness, cut off from everyone and everything? Not because you wanted to? Because you were forced to?

That wasn't something he would wish on any woman.

"I just need to eat, I think. It's been a while, and nursing Ava takes a lot of calories." She sat up, crossing her legs, her skin several shades too pale.

"Did you feed her?" he asked.

"Yes. She's changed, fed and down for a few hours."

"You need to take as good care of yourself as you do of her," he said, helping her out of her coat and hanging it from a hook near the bedroom door. She was still in her boots. Still wearing several layers. She hadn't eaten. Probably hadn't had anything to drink.

"I'm going to make some soup," Poppy offered. "It's canned, but it'll be hot. How about a grilled cheese, too?"

"Soup is fine," Violet said. "But I can make it myself."

"No," Gabe said.

Both women frowned.

"Do either of you really think it's a good idea for her to go up and down the stairs when she just passed out?" he asked, knowing he sounded abrupt and not caring.

He was worried.

Violet was too thin, too pale and too exhausted. She'd fought hard to survive a situation that many people would have found untenable, and it showed.

"He has a point, Violet," Poppy said. "Just relax for a few minutes. I'll be right back with the food."

She hurried away.

Violet was still frowning.

"Should I apologize?" he asked.

"For?"

"Telling you what you can and can't do. Most people aren't thrilled about that."

"I wasn't thinking about that," she admitted, taking off her boots and setting them beside the bed.

"What were you thinking about?"

"How strange it is to be back in a world where it just takes a couple of minutes to make soup. Cooking at the Seavers' took time. We had to get the fire going and bring everything up to temperature."

He lifted a brow. "No propane stove?"

"They had one but didn't like to use it. Propane wasn't sustainable. They couldn't go out into the woods and find it. They had to go to town to buy it. They liked to limit trips to once every couple of months. When I lived there, I'm sure they went more. They were worried about me having enough to eat." She took off the sling she'd carried Ava in, stripped off a thick flannel shirt. Beneath it, she wore a silky, long-sleeved shirt that clung to her slender arms and narrow rib cage.

"Eli has said that the Seavers were always kind to him."

"They were probably kind to everyone before they went off the grid. In all the months I lived with them, I never heard any of them say a mean word about anyone. Maybe that's why they left civilization behind. Maybe they were tired of not getting back what they put out into the world."

"Is that how you feel?" he asked.

She shook her head. "Lance is an exception to all the rules my parents taught me. Most of the people in my life are genuine and warm. They care about me. Not just what I have to offer."

"I'm glad your experience hasn't made you cynical."

"It's made me *cautious*. I certainly don't intend to fall for another handsome face and charming smile. Ava and I will be fine on our own."

"You don't want her to have a father?" he asked, curious to hear her answer. She had what his mother hadn't—financial security and the support of a community of friends.

She hesitated, glancing at the crib. "I want her to have a life filled with love, security, faith and hope. I had two parents, and that was wonderful, but I don't think she'll be ruined forever if she doesn't have a father figure in her life. I hope." She bit her lower lip, a frown line appearing between her brows.

Obviously, she was worried.

No parent wanted to think they were shortchanging their child.

"She'll be fine," he assured her.

"I hope you're right."

"I turned out fine, and my father was never in my life. I didn't have a mother after the age of seven. That's when she passed away and I was placed in foster care."

She met his eyes, and he could see the compassion in her eyes, the sorrow for his losses. "I'm sorry, Gabe. I can't imagine how tough that must have been for you."

"It was fine. I learned to take care of myself at a young age. It's served me well, and now I do a lot of work with kids in the community who don't have fathers in their lives." He smiled, not wanting her to think he dwelled in the past or mourned what he'd hadn't had.

"Do you want children of your own one day?"

He almost said no, but he glanced at Ava, sleeping in the crib, her cheeks pink, her downy hair curling around her tiny ears.

"A few weeks ago, I might have said no, but Ava has won me over. She's a sweet baby. I guess I'll see what God does and not rule anything out."

"I never thought I wanted a dog," she replied with a smile. "But then I met Bear."

"Seems we both may have changed our minds about a few things," he said, tucking a strand of her hair behind her ear. "Who knows what we could change our minds about next?"

"I'm not going to change my mind about enjoying the trappings of civilized life," she said with a quiet laugh. "I like having a bed and a real floor and windows."

"Me, too, but I thought I liked being a loner. Doing

the bachelor thing, just me and Bear, but maybe I'm changing my mind about that, too. It's not a bad thing having companionship."

"It depends on who the companion is and what he or she wants from you."

"Sometimes, a companion wants nothing except your company." He touched her cheek, his hand lingering on smooth warm flesh before dropping to her shoulder. He could imagine a future with her and Ava in it, and if he hadn't been afraid of scaring her away, he'd have told her that.

She studied his face, looking for whatever truth she thought she'd find there. "My father always said it was good to be open-minded, to not close yourself off to possibilities and to allow yourself to go wherever God leads."

"That's excellent advice."

"It is. Maybe when this is all over, we should both follow it."

She might have responded to that. She looked like she was going to, but the door opened.

"Soup's ready," Poppy said, stepping into the room with a tray. Her gaze landed on Gabe's hand, still sitting on Violet's shoulder.

She smirked but didn't comment.

"I brought you crackers and cheese, too. Also some fruit. You need to nourish yourself if you're going to nourish your baby."

"Thank you," Violet said, taking the tray and setting it on the bedside table. "I appreciate it."

"The patrol officers are here, Gabe. You planning on going to the motel with the K-9 team? We're hoping to track Lance from the room, maybe figure out where else he might be holing up."

"Yes, I'm coming." He called to Bear, letting his hand drop away from Violet.

He didn't want to leave her or Ava. That was the sharpest thought in his mind. He wanted to stay with them, make certain they had what they needed and were well guarded. But they'd never be safe until Lance was apprehended.

He'd run from Violet's home, gotten in a car and escaped again, but he couldn't escape forever. Eventually he'd be caught.

Gabe would do everything in his power to make sure that happened.

ELEVEN

Nearly two weeks after moving into the safe house, Violet was finally adjusting to life back in the civilized world.

Not that there had been a whole lot of adjusting to do. Living in the cabin was as easy as living in the bunker had been difficult.

Hot showers every day.

Hot meals any time.

Lights.

Heat.

Music, if she wanted it.

Violet had found a piano in an alcove off the hearth room, and she played nearly every day. Gabe had brought her sheet music and a hymnal from his church.

In the evenings, he'd hold Ava while Violet played through some of her favorites.

Light streamed through the windows, warming the hardwood floors, and the newborn had plenty of time to lie on the blankets on the floor or sit in the baby swing one of the K-9 officers had brought.

It was a good place to be. But Violet still longed for home.

Each day, when Gabe returned from work, she asked if they were any closer to finding Lance. His response was always the same—they were working on it.

Lance had disappeared.

The same way he had after he and Jared were questioned by the police. He hadn't made an appearance since he'd gone after her at her house. There'd been no sightings and no leads.

Some of the K-9 officers had questioned whether he was still alive.

Violet thought he was. His sense of self-importance and self-preservation were too strong for him to have taken many risks.

"It's going to be okay, love," she murmured against Ava's hair. Despite eating well, she was still tiny, and Violet was beginning to worry that she wasn't thriving. She had a well-baby checkup scheduled for the following day but had been hesitating to bring it up to the police.

It was a big deal to take her out of her hiding place. If she left, she risked Lance finding her again. But if Ava wasn't healthy, that was another risk.

One Violet wasn't willing to take.

She paced her bedroom, listening to the muted voices of the patrol officers who were stationed at the house during the day.

At night, Gabe and one of the other K-9 officers took turns patrolling the area with their dogs. She had gotten used to having them around. But there was something *more* with Gabe.

Violet wasn't just used to him. She enjoyed his company. Looked forward to his return. And she made certain she was awake in the morning to say goodbye when he left for the day.

He had become part of her life.

Someone whom she counted on for advice, for conversation, for laughter. She hadn't been allowed to see Ariel. She'd called her friends and texted them, but she couldn't sit face-to-face, looking them in the eyes.

Gabe had filled the gap, his strength, kindness and faith drawing her in.

She grabbed a fresh diaper and changed Ava, frowning at the thinness of her arms and legs.

Weren't babies supposed to be chubby? Shouldn't they have rolls on their thighs and dimples on their knuckles? The thought that something was horribly wrong with Ava had settled deep in the pit of her stomach, and she couldn't stop thinking about it.

Her phone buzzed, and she glanced at the text, smiling when she realized it was Gabe.

Checking in. How are you and Sweet Girl? Need anything from the store? he asked.

I'm worried, she typed quickly, afraid if she didn't say it, she'd decide not to. She didn't want to endanger herself or anyone else, but she also didn't want to neglect her daughter's health and well-being.

About?

Ava. I'm afraid she isn't gaining weight.

Have you called the doctor?

She has an appointment with the midwife tomorrow at 9:00 a.m.

Okay. I'll get it set up set up with the team so we can get you both there safely. We'll talk when I get home.

Home. The place where love lived. Where people felt safe and happy and accepted. She'd had that growing up…then lost it when her parents died. She had thought she had found it again with Lance, but he had never made her feel like Gabe did. As if he had her back. No matter what. As if he wouldn't just fight for her, he'd fight *with* her.

Her phone rang, and she glanced at the number, hoping it was the Seavers. She's been calling every day, but the family had one cell phone that they only used when they left the bunker. Harrison had made her memorize the number the first time she'd gone to the medical clinic. She'd borrowed the clinic's phone to call him and let him know she was ready to return to the bunker.

Unfortunately, when the phone wasn't being used, it was turned off. Cole worried his family could be tracked, and their lives could be upended, if he kept it on.

She hadn't been able to reach them, but she still kept hoping they'd somehow reach out to her.

They had to be frantic with worry.

As much as she had longed to return to town, she couldn't deny how kind the Seavers had been or how accepted they'd made her feel. She didn't want to cause them trouble or stress, but the number on her caller ID wasn't theirs. It didn't belong to anyone she knew.

It could have been anyone wanting anything, but her skin crawled and she tensed, waiting to see if whoever it was left a message.

Lance wasn't patient.

He didn't believe in letting life happen.

He went out and got what he wanted.

Someone knocked on the bedroom door, and she jumped, her heart in her throat as she hurried to open it.

Trooper Hunter McCord stood in the hall, his husky beside him. K-9 officer Will Stryker was a few feet away, a small border collie at his side.

"Sorry to bother you," Hunter said. "I hope we didn't disturb the baby."

"She's sleeping," Violet responded, stepping into the hall. "What's going on?"

Had something happened to Gabe? Had he been injured after he'd texted? Had Lance somehow hurt him? The thought filled her with dread.

"We came on the behalf of one of our team members. Eli Partridge. He works the tech side of our investigations," Will explained.

"We've met."

"Did he mention his connection to Bettina Seaver?" Trooper Stryker asked.

"Yes. He wanted information about where the Seavers are living, but I can't give it to him."

"Bettina is critically ill," Trooper Stryker said.

As he spoke, his dog cocked his head and looked up at him, totally focused and alert, ready for any command. "She may not survive the next few weeks, and her dying wish is to see her son and his family."

"I'm sorry about that. I have deep sympathy for Bettina, but—"

"Hear me out." He cut her off. "Harrison Seaver walked into the police department to ask if we had any information on you. He wouldn't give us much regarding how he knew you. He just said he had reason to be concerned. He'd already been to the local hospitals."

"I've been trying to contact them. I knew they'd be wondering what happened to me."

"We assured him that you're safe, and then we asked him to wait at the station while we met with you," Trooper Stryker told her. "We think that if you write a letter to Cole asking him to visit his mother, he might capitulate and agree."

"As I explained to Eli, I did discuss this with Cole. Harrison and I tried to get him to put aside whatever bad feelings he has, but he dug in his heels and refused."

"Did he say why he's upset with his mother?" Hunter interjected.

"No, and I'm not even sure it's just about his mom. He worries about going back to town and getting caught up in the kind of life he left behind. Cole eschewed all the trappings of modern life, and I wonder if he thinks that going back will remind him and his family of what they left behind."

"She's still his mother," Hunter said. "There has to be some part of him that wants to reach out before she dies."

"Maybe, but even if I thought I could convince him, there's no way he'd ever believe I wrote the letter. He'd believe you did it to try to draw him into to town. Cole can be little…conspiracy theorist. He doesn't trust anyone he doesn't know."

Trooper Stryker frowned. "What if you gave the letter to Harrison? Would Cole believe it then?"

"Probably," Violet said. Cole trusted the people who were close to him. Everyone else was subject to suspicion.

"Can we do it?" he asked, shifting his gaze to Hunter.

"We can do it. I'm just trying to decide if it's a good move with Lance still at large. Let's discuss it with the rest of the team," Hunter suggested. "Do you mind waiting here for a few minutes?" he asked Violet.

"Not at all," she replied, wondering where he thought she would go. There were police stationed inside and outside the house. Every time she even looked at an exterior door, one appeared.

"We'll be back in a moment."

The men walked downstairs, and she returned to her room.

Ava was still sleeping, her chest rising and falling gently.

She seemed more comfortable and content since they'd left the bunker. If only she would start gaining weight, Violet could stop worrying.

She touched her daughter's cheek, imagining what their relationship would be like in the future. She couldn't fathom a rift so wide and deep they never spoke, never visited, never spent time together. Just the thought was enough to nearly break her heart.

Violet walked back into the hall.

She could hear voices and the quiet patter of dog feet

on the floor. She still didn't think writing a letter would change Cole's mind, but she had to try.

She opened the desk drawer, found a piece of paper and pen, then sat down and started to write.

The afternoon sky was deep azure, sprinkled with white clouds, the sun bright and warm as Gabe returned to the safe house. The log structure was tucked neatly among tall pine trees, mountains looming behind it. It was a picturesque location, far from the main road and hidden from view. A nice place to stay, but he knew Violet was getting restless. She wanted to return to her childhood home and her life.

He could understand that, but his goal was to make sure she and Ava remained safe. In his opinion, that meant staying hidden here until Lance was apprehended.

No excursions into town except for emergencies.

Ava's doctor's appointment was an emergency.

Bringing a letter to Harrison Seaver at the police station was not. The team had deemed it low risk. Lance hadn't made an appearance in two weeks. No sightings. No leads. As far as anyone knew, he'd left town.

Maybe he had.

Maybe murdering his best friend in front of a police officer had made him flee Alaska.

Gabe doubted it.

A guy who had stuck around for seven months wasn't going to change his MO. He'd continue to hunt his prey, lying low until he sighted her again.

Bringing Violet into town gave him that opportunity, and that was something Gabe wasn't comfortable with.

He'd made his misgivings known, but the team had everything in place to keep her safe. Four K-9 team members would escort her to and from the precinct. Several patrol officers would stay with Ava.

The dirt road leading to the safe house was three miles long and stretched through private property. Ava was safe with at the house with patrol officers. No one but the team and patrol officers should be on it. If Lance spotted Violet in Anchorage and attempted to follow her back to the safe house, he'd be seen, and he'd be stopped.

But Gabe was still concerned.

He had gotten close to Violet during the weeks he'd been staying at the safe house. He'd watched her with Ava, listened to her play piano and hum old hymns, heard stories about her childhood and her parents. They'd spent late nights chatting about life, about faith and about all the things that they each valued.

Surprisingly, the two of them had more in common than he would ever have believed possible.

He and Violet both valued family and friendship, hard work and integrity. They enjoyed being home but also enjoyed the outdoors. No bars. No late-night outings. None of the things so many people their age seemed to gravitate toward.

Additionally, they both were invested in the community.

Violet had mentioned helping to expand the medical clinic where she had gotten pre- and postnatal care. She had said she had the means and the business acumen, and he had no doubt she'd accomplish anything she set her mind to.

He admired that.

He admired *her*, his feelings deeper and stronger than he should have been comfortable with. Even though he had lived the last few years as a die-hard bachelor, he didn't play the field. He wasn't that kind of guy. But after his engagement ended, he'd gone out with a few women over the years, enjoying their company but never allowing the relationship to go deeper than surface connections.

He was past that point with Violet.

They had bonded their first night together, when they'd sat out the storm, waiting and wondering if Lance would show up.

That bond had continued to grow, and he couldn't imagine a future where they weren't friends, where they didn't spend evenings in front of a roaring fire, taking turns rocking Ava while they talked...

Gabe sighed. He had a job to do and he'd better get on with it. He got out of the SUV, opening the back hatch and offering Bear a bowl of water. There was no sense getting him out. They'd be leaving as soon as Violet was ready.

"Gabe!" Hunter called, stepping out the front door and hurrying toward him. "We've got everything in place at the precinct. Violet has finished writing the letter, and Harrison Seaver had agreed to carry it to Cole. We should be leaving shortly."

"You know my feelings about this," he said, scratching Bear behind the ears as the dog lapped up the last of the water.

"I understand your misgivings, but we've thought

this through, and I've run it by the colonel. The only way Cole is going to believe that letter is from Violet is if someone he trusts assures him that it is. Harrison can let him know she delivered the letter under no duress. The colonel agrees this is low risk, and we're not putting Violet or Harrison in danger. The likelihood Lance is hanging out near the police station is minuscule."

"I agree, but I'm still not comfortable with taking Violet out when it's not necessary. Ava has an appointment at the medical clinic tomorrow, and we're going to have to bring them to town for that. Why not ask Harrison to meet us there tomorrow?"

"There's snow in the forecast for the morning, and he's coming on foot from somewhere in the park. He may not make it. Is there any way Violet can get the baby in this afternoon? We can bring Harrison to the clinic and have her hand him the letter there."

"I can ask," Gabe said. He would still rather not bring Violet into town at all, but she was worried about Ava's growth and development, and a medical checkup couldn't be put off.

He texted her, asking if the medical clinic could see Ava a day early. Minutes later, she responded with an affirmative. She'd get the baby ready and be out shortly.

"She can bring her daughter today," he said, tucking his phone into his pocket and meeting Hunter's eyes. "I know the team is hopeful that Lance has moved on and left the area, but hopes don't keep people safe. We're going to need a K-9 team in front of the clinic and one in back. Do we have some patrol officers who can run cars past the address?"

"I'll get it set up. I know you're worried, Gabe, but

the team is strong and capable. Violet and Ava will be fine."

"I know," he agreed.

He planned to make certain of it.

TWELVE

Violet was terrified, her stomach a jumble of knots that she couldn't dispel. She tried to focus on the scenery—the gorgeous mountain views and the pristine sky. It was a beautiful fall day, the air crisp without being too cold. In a few weeks, the ground would be coated with snow, but for now there was still a carpet of green beneath a layer of fall leaves.

She loved Anchorage in every season. Snow-peaked mountains, rain-shrouded summer, spring flowers and colorful fall days. She wanted to raise Ava with the same appreciation, introducing her to the outdoor activities that she'd spent her childhood involved in.

But first, they had to get through this tumultuous season.

"You okay?" Gabe asked as he pulled onto the main road that led into Anchorage.

"Just a little nervous."

"A *little*? You're digging holes in your palms." He touched her hand, smoothing his palm over her fisted knuckles.

"Okay. I'm a lot nervous," she admitted, opening her hand and letting the blood flow back into her fingers.

"That's understandable. To be honest, I wasn't excited about bringing you to town this afternoon. My priority is your and Ava's safety. I have all kinds of sympathy for Bettina Seaver, but I don't want to risk your life to try to convince a man to do something he has already refused to be part of." He wove his fingers through hers, holding her hand as he navigated the two-lane highway.

She didn't tug away or question the warmth that spread through her at his touch. "Is that why you asked if I could bring Ava to the clinic today?"

"Yes. Getting her checked out is a priority. If we can do both things today, we won't have to take risks tomorrow."

"I hope she's okay." She glanced at Ava, tucked into an infant car seat and sleeping soundly. "I had most of my prenatal care, but not all of it. If I harmed her by—"

"Violet, you did everything you could for her. You're still doing everything you can. If there's something wrong, and I don't think there is, it has nothing to do with anything you have or haven't done." He gave her hand a gentle squeeze and offered a quick smile.

Her heart leaped in response, her body humming with sweet contentment and a gentle longing for things she had stopped believing she could have. Love, companionship, friendship and passion had been the cornerstones of her parents' relationship. She had been looking for those things when she'd met Lance. He had allowed her to think she'd found them.

Now that she'd spent time with Gabe, she understood that what he'd offered had been a pale facsimile of the real deal. Lance's friendship had been one-sided, his passion selfish and his love and companionship offered with strings attached.

Gabe asked for nothing. Demanded nothing. Over and over again, he had proven he cared selflessly.

She couldn't help being smitten by that.

By *him*.

"I wish I'd met you sooner," she blurted, the words slipping out before she realized she was going to say them. "I'm sorry. I shouldn't have said that," she added quickly, embarrassed for herself, for the neediness she felt when she was with Gabe.

She'd always prided herself on her independence.

But there was a piece of her heart that did need the handsome trooper—his quiet strength, his confidence, his easy companionship. She craved that the way she craved sunshine after a long Alaska winter.

"Why?" he asked quietly, still holding her hand.

Anchorage was in front of them, the city sprawling out across the landscape. They'd be at the medical clinic soon. Violet had been told how things would go down—she'd be escorted in by Gabe. There would be patrol officers on the street, K-9 officers outside. Lance wasn't going to get a chance to harm her or the baby. Not if the state police had anything to say about it.

Yet she was still afraid.

"Why am I sorry I said it?" she asked, her stomach flip-flopping as they drove past a restaurant where she and Lance had once eaten.

"Yeah. Why do you wish you'd met me sooner?"

"If I had, none of this would have happened. Lance never would have been part of my life. Two people wouldn't be dead. Ariel wouldn't have been hurt."

"You wouldn't have Ava," he pointed out.

She nodded. "I wouldn't trade her for a do-over, but... I feel tainted by Lance. I didn't realize how much of myself I'd given away until after I spent time with the Seavers."

"You didn't give it away. You put it on a shelf for a while. Now you've taken it down again. Which is good. I like the person you are. Your integrity. Your kindness. Your enthusiasm for the community and the people in it. Your strength." He lifted her hand and kissed her knuckles, the gesture sweet and surprising.

"If I were strong, Lance never would have taken advantage of me."

"Cut yourself some slack. Your parents hadn't been gone long. You were vulnerable, and like any predator, Lance can sense that in people." His gaze shifted to the rearview mirror as they entered downtown Anchorage.

Four K-9 vehicles were behind them, each containing a trooper and a dog, ready and willing to do whatever it took to keep Violet and Ava safe.

She couldn't put into words how that made her feel. That they would risk so much for a stranger touched her in a way not many things had.

She would find a way to thank them.

When this was over, she'd donate to the K-9 development program, but she wanted to do something more personal, too.

"Thanksgiving is coming," she said, her heart in her throat as Gabe turned onto the road that led to the clinic.

"Just a couple weeks away," he agreed.

"I was thinking, if Lance is behind bars by then, we

could have a Thanksgiving celebration for your team. I've got plenty of room at my house to host everyone."

"That sounds nice," he said, pulling up in front of the clinic and parking the SUV. "But we're talking a lot of dogs and a lot of people. Your house may never be the same."

"I don't want it to be," she replied. "I want my first memories after this is over to be of people enjoying the home my parents built, filling it up with laughter and conversation and love."

He nodded, looking into her eyes, studying her face, his expression soft. "You're a special person, Violet. Someone I'm glad to know."

"I'm glad to know you, too," she said.

"Good." He smiled, leaning close, his lips brushing hers. A surprise, but not. They had been moving toward each other from the moment they'd met.

The tenderness of the kiss, the sweetness of the gesture, made her heart ache.

If she had to put a name to it, she'd have called it love. But was she truly ready to take a leap of faith with this man after everything she'd been through?

"Ready?" he asked, squeezing her hand as he broke away.

"As I'll ever be," she responded.

"Bear and I are going to escort you inside. Harrison is already there. Once he has the letter, he's taking off and you'll go back for Ava's appointment. I'll be in the waiting area. Trooper West and his dog, Grace, are stationed by the back door. If things go south, one of us will get you out of there."

"Okay," she said, her voice shaky, her hands trembling as she unhooked Ava's car seat.

"It's going to be okay, Violet," Gabe said.

She hoped he was right.

Prayed he was.

Because more than anything, she wanted this to be over.

She wanted to go home so she could get back to the world she'd left behind. And she wanted the Thanksgiving celebration she'd described, with all the K-9 team members and their dogs filling the empty house.

Just four walls and a roof if you don't have love to fill it.

That had been her parents' motto and the reason they'd opened their home so frequently. Neither had wanted to squander the blessings that God had poured out on them. They'd wanted to share with those they cared about, and they'd often hosted parties for hospital staff and for business associates.

She hadn't followed in their footsteps.

After they died, she'd moved back into the house, but she hadn't filled it the way they had. She hadn't brought in friends and coworkers or practiced the hospitality her parents had so clearly demonstrated.

Violet wanted to change that.

Because deep down, she desperately wanted to have a second chance at creating something wonderful out of the tragedy she'd suffered.

"Stay here until I open your door," Gabe said as he got out of the SUV.

She waited while he freed Bear.

There were a few people around. Walking on the

sidewalk or getting into cars. None looked like Lance, but that didn't mean he wasn't nearby.

Her heart was racing frantically when Gabe opened the door.

He lifted the infant seat and stepped back, his gaze on the street and the surrounding areas. Bear seemed relaxed, his tongue lolling out, his tail high. If there was trouble nearby, he didn't sense it. Across the street, a patrol car pulled into a parking lot, the marked vehicle idling there. Would Lance dare make an appearance with so many police nearby? She prayed not.

Gabe hurried her into the clinic. The waiting room was nearly empty. Just two people sitting in chairs, staring at the television mounted to the wall.

Two others stood near the front windows. One of them was Trooper Maya Rodriguez and her dog, Sarge. Beside the female K-9 officer was a tall, lanky teenager who was as familiar as sunshine and a sight for sore eyes.

"Harrison!" Violet cried, running to greet the young man who had become as close to her as a brother. "I'm so sorry that I worried you and your family. I tried to call, but you know how hard it is to get through."

"I do, and it's okay," he said, giving her an awkward hug. "The police explained what happened. I'm glad you and Ava are okay."

"How are your parents?" she asked as Gabe stepped up beside her. His presence was comforting. Just knowing he was there made her feel as if everything would work out. He was an anchor in the storm, a steadiness she desperately needed.

"The same. Although, now that you're gone, Mom

seems a little…sad. I guess that's the right word. With you there, she wasn't alone when Dad and I went hunting and fishing. Without you, I guess she's realized how lonely it can get out there."

"I'm sorry, hon."

"For what? You didn't cause it. Our lifestyle did. To be honest, I feel sorry for her, but I'm also hoping it might be the catalyst that brings us back to town. You know how Dad is. He's stubborn, but he'll do anything to make her happy." He grinned.

"I know, but if they stay out there, remember what I said—my doors are always open. If you want to attend college, you'll have a place to stay."

"Thanks, Violet. I'm planning to take you up on that. I went to the library earlier today and filled out a few college applications."

"Good for you! You're going to keep me updated on your progress, right?"

"You know it." He glanced out the window. "It's getting late. I'm going to need to start back now if I'm going to be back before dark. "

"Right. This is for your dad. I included my cell phone number so he can get in touch with me if he wants to discuss things." Violet pulled out the letter she'd written. She'd poured out her heart to Cole, explaining how heartbroken she'd be if she were in his mother's position. She could only hope that inspired him to change his mind.

"I'll pass it on to him. Hopefully he'll decide to visit Gram. I haven't seen her since I was a baby, and I don't want to miss out on getting to know her." He folded the letter and zipped it into his pocket.

"Be careful on your way home," she said, knowing there was no need to caution him. He was aware of the dangers, and he knew how to avoid them.

True to his nature, he nodded politely. "You know I will. I'll try to call you the next time I'm in town."

He leaned down to kiss Ava on the cheek.

"Tell your parents I said hello and thank you."

"I will." He waved and walked out the door.

Confident for his age.

Self-assured.

She wanted so much for him and for his family.

The door to the treatment area opened, and a nurse peered into the waiting room. "Vivian and Annie," she called, using the phony names Violet had provided.

"Right here." Violet grabbed the car seat carrier and met Gabe's eyes. "This shouldn't be long."

"I'll be out here when you finish. If anything goes wrong, stay in the exam room and wait for me to come for you."

Violet didn't ask what could go wrong. She'd seen what Lance was capable of. He knew how to set fires, to track through snow, to find her when she didn't think she could be found.

"I will," she said, praying it wouldn't come to that.

She wanted the appointment to go smoothly, and she wanted everyone to get back to the safe house without incident or injury.

The nurse led her to an exam room at the end of the hall, the back exit just yards away. If she had to, Violet could take Ava out that way. There were police patrolling the streets, K-9 officers inside and outside.

She had to believe that everything was going to be okay.

Lifting Ava from the carrier, she removed her coat and knit cap. She'd just set her back in the carrier when the door flew open.

The nurse was there, pale faced and terrified, a man beside her. Dark hair. Thick glasses. A beard.

Holding a gun.

It took her a second too long to realize whom she was looking at.

Lance!

"Do not make a sound, or I will shoot this woman and kill your baby before I kill you," he growled, his eyes flashing with hatred.

"She's your baby, too," she said, her voice shaking with fear.

"Do you think I care? I didn't want a baby. That's why you hid the pregnancy from me. You're a liar and a thief!"

He was dressed in scrubs, a stethoscope around his neck, and she could only imagine that he'd faked his credentials and taken a job working for the clinic.

He had known she would bring Ava there for check-ups, and he had made sure that he would have access to both of them.

"What do you want?" she asked, her voice raspy, her heart beating wildly.

He grinned. "Everything. You wouldn't give me the two million, so now you'll give me every dime. Grab the baby and let's go."

She wouldn't allow him to have Ava.

"She'll slow us down. And with all the police outside—"

"Shut up!" He grabbed her arm, yanking her to his

side and pressing the gun to her temple. "I make the decisions."

"She's right. A baby is going to slow you down and draw attention to you," the nurse said, her voice shaking as she stepped between Lance and the car seat. She was obviously trying to protect Ava, and Violet could have cried with gratitude.

Lance pointed the gun at the nurse's head and removed the safety.

She flinched, and he laughed.

"How about you stay out of our business?" He put the safety back on then turned back to Violet. "Fine, the baby can stay, but you and I are outta here. Come on, let's go."

He dragged Violet into the hall.

She wanted to break free and run, but she knew he'd kill her and anyone who tried to stop him if she did.

They were at the back door in seconds, outside in the bright sunlight.

She heard a dog growl, saw an officer lying near the street. Sean West. She recognized his blond hair and his beautiful Akita, Grace. She barked wildly, her lead caught underneath his prone body.

"What did you do?" she gasped.

"Just hit him over the head. He wasn't expecting a doctor to attack." Lance chuckled maniacally. "Now, stop worrying about him, and start worrying about yourself. Move!"

Violet thought Sean moved as they hurried past. She wanted to go to him, jerked sideways trying to help.

"Move it!" Lance snapped, dragging her across the road.

Sirens were blaring.

Another dog barked.

She glanced back, saw Bear and Gabe running out the back door of the clinic.

"Stop! Police!" Gabe shouted, but Lance had made it to the corner of the street, and he dragged her into a parking garage, shoving her toward a stairwell.

"Move faster or you're going to die right here," he snarled.

She bounded up the stairs, breathless with terror, grief-stricken over what had happened to Trooper West.

Please, spare his life, she prayed.

"This way!" Lance grabbed her ponytail, yanking her sideways toward the third floor of the lot.

A beat-up green pickup truck sat in a stream of sunlight near the exit ramp.

He shoved her toward it, and she fell, sprawling on her hands and knees and sliding across the concrete floor, her jeans ripping, her hands bloodied.

"Get up!" He dragged her to her feet, shoving her into the now-open driver's side door of the truck. She climbed into the seat, desperate to find a way out.

He had the gun pointed at her head, his gaze cold and hard. "Scoot over. I'll drive. Just like old times."

"What do you want, Lance?"

"I already told you, and it isn't about what I want. It's about what I'm going to *have*. After all you've put me through these last few months, you owe me."

Sirens blared, strobe lights flashing as a patrol car raced into the parking garage.

Lance swore, opening the door and dragging her back out of the car. "See this!" he shrieked. "See the trouble you've caused! I had it all planned out, and you ruined everything!"

She didn't speak, she didn't want to waste her breath or risk riling him up more.

"We need another exit. We can't take those stairs," he muttered, rushing toward the other stairwell, the gun pressed to her side as he forced her along.

They headed up another four levels.

Dogs were barking below, the sound echoing hollowly through the structure.

Was Gabe there? Following Bear through the maze of vehicles? Her heart jumped at the thought, her soul aching to see him, to have the comfort of knowing he was there.

She thought she'd known what love was, and then she'd met Gabe. He was everything she had ever wanted, every dream she'd ever had. That he had come into her life when she'd needed him most didn't surprise her. God had known exactly who and exactly when and exactly how. And He knew this moment. He was in control. She had to believe that.

They reached the top level, sunlight streaming down from the pristine sky. Mountain and water views. Snow-capped peaks.

A perfect day in Anchorage, and she didn't plan to die. Not when she had so much to live for.

She glanced around, searching for a weapon or an escape route. She was desperate to see Gabe but terrified of the danger he would face if he appeared. She needed to act before Lance had a chance to hurt anyone else.

"What are you doing?" Lance barked, shoving the gun against her cheek, his eyes wild.

"Looking for a way out," she replied honestly.

"The only way out is down. You want to go first?" he asked, pushing her backward against the exterior wall, her ponytail dangling into open air. A little more effort on his part and she'd be over the side, falling to the ground.

The second stairwell was to their left, a fire extinguisher attached to the wall nearby.

If she could reach it, she could use it.

"We can take the other stairs. The police are stupid. They'll expect you to be leaving in a vehicle. Their dogs are following us up, but they won't know we're heading back down." She tried to sound confident and helpful rather than desperate.

Lance scowled, easing back so that she was no longer hanging over the wall. "Don't try to fool me, Violet. I don't like it."

"I'm not doing anything except trying to get out of this alive. If you want my money, you can have it. We just have to get to a safe place so I can transfer everything."

"Right. Let's go." He yanked her away from the ledge, shoved her toward the stairwell.

She went. Eyes focused on the fire extinguisher, body numb with fear.

She could hear the dogs. They were getting closer. What would Lance do if they appeared? Would he shoot the dogs? Would he shoot her? Use her as a shield? He had been willing to kill his own child. He wouldn't hesitate to kill Violet.

She reached the stairwell. The fire extinguisher was right there! *Do it!* her mind shouted.

She pretended to stumble, her hands hitting cement, then feeling the cool metal of the canister.

"Hurry up!" Lance yelled, grabbing her arm.

She had the extinguisher in her hand, and praying for the strength she desperately needed, she swung around, slamming it into his face.

The gun went off, the shot pinging into the wall beside her.

A man shouted.

She didn't hear what he said.

Because she was running, sprinting down the stairs, taking them two and three at a time, Lance cursing viciously as he followed.

"They're heading back down!" Brayden Ford shouted into the radio. He and his Newfoundland, Ella, had made it to the top floor of the parking garage just ahead of Gabe.

"Who fired the shot?" Hunter responded, his voice tight with tension. Sean had been hit over the head and knocked unconscious by Lance. He was up and moving, talking and coherent, but the team was still concerned for his welfare.

"The perp. Our victim hit him in the face with a fire extinguisher," Brayden answered. "They are in the stairwell."

"Let's go get them. I want to take this guy down and put him in jail where he belongs," Gabe said, adrenaline coursing through him as he passed the abandoned fire extinguisher.

There was blood on the cement stairs. Drops of it leading down. Had Violet been injured? Or had Lance?

Bear snuffled the air and shook out his fur, a habit he had when he was getting close to a scent source.

They reached the third floor at a dead run, and Gabe expected to continue down. Instead, Bear loped into the garage, Ella right beside him.

"What do you think?" Brayden asked, scanning the area.

"She made it down here and hid. He heard us coming and did the same."

There were dozens of cars lined up in rows. Plenty of places for the perp to hide.

"I don't know about you, but I don't want to risk my dog. Ella's not trained for this, and this guy has already proven that he has no conscience," Brayden said grimly. "He'll shoot anyone or anything who gets in his way."

"I feel the same. Let's text this in. I don't know how close he is, and I don't want him to hear radio comms. We'll have the team stationed on level two of all stairwells. Helena and Luna on the way up. When they get here, we'll have the advantage. If he tries to get out the parking garage, he'll be caught."

But Gabe had a feeling he wouldn't try to escape. Not without Violet. He wanted her money, and he wanted revenge.

Both were powerful motivators.

"Lance! Police! Throw down your weapon and come out with your hands where we can see them!" he commanded, calling Bear back with a hand signal and putting him in a down-stay position.

He wouldn't move again until he was told.

No response from Lance, but Bear's head swiveled, his dark eyes focused on some cars near an exterior wall.

"I said come out!" Gabe repeated, motioning for Brayden to break to the left.

He'd head right.

Lance couldn't take them both out at once.

Bear growled, the warning making the hair on Gabe's arms stand on end. He dived for cover seconds before a bullet whizzed by.

Lance appeared to his right, gun raised and pointed.

Not at him.

At Bear.

Gabe raised his weapon, would have fired, but Violet darted out from behind a van, throwing herself at Lance and knocking him off his feet.

"Police! Surrender or I'll send in my dog!" Helena shouted as she raced out of the stairwell.

Luna was on a lead, snarling wildly.

The world was chaotic, everyone in motion. Violet struggling to break free. Lance dragging her to her feet, pressing a gun to head.

Everything suddenly went silent and still.

For a heartbeat no one moved. Even the dogs were quiet.

Sirens blared from below.

Feet pounded on cement stairs, but this part of the garage seemed held in a strange tableau, caught in a spell that prevented action. Three dogs and their handlers standing with guns drawn.

The perp fifty yards away, a gun pressed to Violet's temple.

The sound of traffic and pedestrians drifted in on the cold wind, a reminder that life was playing out all around them while they stood still, held hostage by the moment.

"Everyone, back off!" Lance snapped, blood pouring from his nose and dripping onto the floor.

Violet was pale but seemed uninjured, her eyes wide and filled with terror. Gabe wanted to reassure her. He wanted to tell her that everything was going to be okay. He wanted to tell her how much she meant to him, how deeply he cared for her and for Ava and how important they were in his life, but his focus had to be on getting the gun out of Lance's hand.

"I said back off!" Lance bellowed, his voice echoing off the cement walls. His eyes were wild, his free arm wrapped around Violet's upper body, locking her close to his chest.

Using her as a shield. Like the coward he was.

"Let's all give him some space," Helena suggested, shifting back a few feet.

Gabe and Brayden did the same. Let him relax and think he was winning. Cockiness would lead to mistakes. Once he made one, they'd have him.

"That's it," Lance muttered. "That's better. Just stay back and no one has to get hurt."

He dragged Violet back a few feet, moving toward the cement wall that opened out onto the street.

"Put the weapon down," Gabe said. "You know you can't get out of here."

"I can do whatever I want. Haven't I proven that already? You and your team have been looking for me for months, and you've never once gotten close to finding me. Ironic, since you've got those dogs out searching for missing people all the time." He laughed, the sound harsh and erratic.

"We have you now," Helena said. "How about you admit it and stop fighting?"

"Why would I want to do that?" He sneered. "I've always loved a good fight. I've always been really good at winning them."

He reached the wall, glanced down as if contemplating jumping.

The thought made Gabe's blood run cold.

If he went over, would he try to take Violet with him?

"Here's how things are going to work," Lance said. "I'm going to give you and your friends five minutes to clear my path out of here. Then I'll to take my lovely lady and we'll walk down the stairs and out onto the street. If any of your buddies or their dogs try to stop me, I'll shoot Violet and will kill every civilian I see."

He glanced at his watch.

"Tell you what. I'm a generous guy. I'll give you six minutes. Starting now."

He pressed the gun firmer into Violet's temple and smiled.

Lance wouldn't get what he wanted, but Gabe would allow him to think he was in charge.

He lifted his radio and called in the request for all officers to stand down.

THIRTEEN

Lance loved to be in control.

Violet had realized that soon after meeting him, but it hadn't set off alarm bells. After all, her father had always been a take-charge kind of guy, and she hadn't seen that as a negative attribute.

However, Lance didn't just take charge. He forced people to do his bidding.

His import-export business had floundered because everyone he hired quit. The only good friend he had was Jared.

Had been Jared.

Most people couldn't abide his arrogant assumption that his way was the *only* way. Violet had made excuses for him, of course. Didn't every person in love do the same? She'd thought Lance needed time to mature, to grow into the role of CEO of his small company. So she'd tried to give him pointers and even lent him cash to help keep his business floating.

He had pretended to listen and acted like he'd appreciated the influx of money. Now she wondered if he had even used it for his business. Not that it mattered.

Because in the grand scheme of all the atrocities Lance had committed, that was drop in the bucket.

"I should have killed you the minute you transferred that money. You've caused me way too much trouble," he muttered as Gabe and two other K-9 officers took a few steps backs. He was arrogant and foolish enough to believe they were really going to let him leave.

Violet knew they wouldn't.

She had to get herself out of his arms and away from his gun. Once she did that, the police could do whatever was necessary to apprehend him. He dragged her back, the gun pressed so hard into her temple she thought the bone might crack.

"Four minutes," he crowed. "I hope they're gone. Violet wasn't planning to die today. Were you, honey?"

"Don't call me that," she spat, hating him for everything he had done.

Hating herself more for what she had allowed.

"Would you rather I call you cupcake or cutie pie? Didn't you love those nicknames when I gave them to you?"

"I hated them."

She'd specifically told him not to call her either. But rather than deterring him, he had made it a point to do so in front of colleagues and business associates.

Another red flag that she had ignored.

"Because you're a boring little bookworm who doesn't like fun things," he grumbled, the gun easing away from her temple. Just a fraction of an inch, but enough to give her hope that he might be losing focus.

"Lance, let her go and we'll clear your path out of

here," Gabe called out. "Otherwise we're sending the dogs after you."

"My dog," Helena Maddox added.

Her Norwegian elkhound growled, eyes laser-sharp focused on Lance.

"That wouldn't be a good idea," Lance responded.

She could feel the shift in him. Like the tide changing course. She'd seen it before. Good humor quickly replaced by rage. He would be in control one minute and out of control the next.

If that happened now, would he kill someone?

She met Gabe's eyes. She could see the calmness in his face, the focus.

"It's okay," he mouthed.

She wanted to believe him, but Lance was dragging her closer to the cement wall again. Three stories down to asphalt and cars. Pedestrians wandering along a sidewalk with no idea that a horrible drama was playing out above them.

It's not okay, she wanted to respond.

"Two minutes, folks, and I'm losing my patience. Is the path clear or not?" Lance shouted.

"I already told you what needs to happen. Release Violet. We'll clear your path to leave." Gabe looked into Violet's eyes, and she could see love there, shining out, asking her to believe that everything would be okay. She wanted to tell him that she did, that she trusted him, that she knew he would come through for her.

"Violet and I are leaving together or she's not leaving at all. We had plans. Big plans. Didn't we, baby doll?"

"I have a name," she replied. "How about you use it?"

"Right, your name. The one that attracted me to you.

I was hoping you'd be more exciting. The only plus side to being with you was that you were easy to manipulate."

It was true.

She had been, but she was stronger now. Wiser. More capable of standing up for herself and the people she loved. And she knew the truth about love and what it felt like. Gabe had taught her that. She met his eyes again, tried to tell him without speaking just how much he meant to her.

"I already told you, I'll give you what I have. Just let me go. I have a baby to go home to," she said, forcing herself to beg, hoping to give Gabe and the K-9 team time to move in.

"You should have thought about that before you took what was mine out of the account."

She wanted to remind him that none of it was his. That he hadn't had a dime to contribute to their house fund, and that he had bought her wedding gift with money she'd provided.

She bit her tongue. She didn't want to poke the tiger. She just wanted to distract him.

"We had an agreement, and I broke it. I understand why you're upset."

"I'm not upset, you little fool. I'm furious. I had tickets to Bangkok and a property I planned to buy that has now been sold to someone else. You ruined everything." He jabbed her with the gun, but it fell farther away from her face as he pulled her to the farthest stairwell.

Gabe and the other troopers were following their progress, watching silently. Inching closer.

She'd seen the subtle movement. One step. Then another. Each of them closing the gap while Lance raged. The elkhound was still on its leash, teeth bared, fangs gleaming.

"Time is up. If the stairwell isn't clear, people die. And, just to prove I mean business, how about I give you a taste of what I'm capable of."

Violet felt his muscles tense and his gun arm shift.

He was planning to shoot. She had no time to shout a warning. He swung the gun toward Bear, but she couldn't let the dog be hurt. She grabbed Lance's arm, yanking it down as he fired. The shot went wild, and so did he.

Turning on her, he slammed the butt of the gun into her cheekbone. The skin split, blood pouring down her face, as he cursed and shoved her backward over the cement wall.

Bowed over, she fought to gain control. The street below was a kaleidoscope of dizzying colors. People shouted commands, but Lance was past hearing.

"Die," he growled, pointing the gun at her face.

Her hand was on his wrist, but she was half over the wall. Nearly falling to the street below.

She had no control.

No way to stop him.

A dog snarled, and Lance screamed, his arm dragged away by the K-9.

Violet scrambled away, blood still pouring from her face as she tried to separate herself from the fray.

The gun clattered onto the ground, skittering a few feet away.

"Off!" Helena commanded.

The dog immediately released its hold on Lance's arm.

"Get on the ground! Now!" Gabe yelled, his gun pointed straight at Lance's heart.

Lance obeyed. Going quietly. A surprise. And, with Lance, surprises were generally not good ones.

Violet was dizzy, off balance and weak. She sat on the ground, leaning against the wall.

A cold nose touched her hand, and she looked into Bear's gentle face. He nuzzled her hair, then settled down beside her.

She had never been a dog person, but Bear wasn't just a dog.

He was a friend, a buddy, a partner.

She touched his head, her hand resting on his velvety fur as Gabe leaned over Lance.

"You have any other weapons on you?" he asked.

"Would I be stupid enough to tell you if I did?" Lance spat.

Gabe frisked him, cuffed him and backed off.

His gaze shifted to Violet, and she could see the fear, anger and relief in his eyes. "Are you okay?"

"Yes. Thanks to you, Bear and the K-9 team." She wanted to throw herself into his arms and hold on until she stopped shaking.

"I've never been that terrified," he admitted, pulling her to her feet and tugging her into his arms. He felt like warmth and safety and home, and she wanted to stand there forever. "And I will never stop being thankful that you're okay."

"I will never stop being thankful for you," she responded.

He pulled back, looking into her face and smiling gently. "You're going to need a few stitches."

"A few stitches are a small price to pay for having him in custody and for putting an end to this nightmare. I'm ready to move on with my life, and I feel like I can finally begin building new dreams," she responded.

"I hope I'm in them," he said.

Her heart swelled. "How could you not be? You've given me a foundation of hope to build those dreams on"

"And, you've helped me believe that the things I dreamed of as a kid could actually be possible—home and family and all the blessings and challenges those bring. Come on. Let's get you to the hospital and get you stitched up. Then, I'll take you home. It's time to start living again."

"My home? Or the safe house?"

"Yours," he replied as Helena yanked Lance to his feet.

Cold air whipped over the wall, ruffling Violet's hair and chilling her skin.

"You people didn't seem to understand the rules of the game," Lance said, his voice monotone, his expression blank. "If I don't get out of here, she doesn't."

He broke free, barreling toward Violet, head down like a battering ram as he tried to throw them both over the wall and onto the street below.

Gabe took milliseconds to respond.

Bear was faster.

One moment he was on the ground. The next, he was launching himself at Lance. His 150-pound body hit like a ton of bricks, throwing Lance sideways and sending him sprawling. Lance was up again in moments, flying toward the wall, scrambling onto it.

"Don't do it!" Gabe commanded. "You still have a trial ahead of you. Plenty of time to prove your innocence."

"We all know I'm not innocent," he exclaimed, his eyes wild with frenetic energy. "And we all know why this all happened."

His gaze shifted to Violet as he teetered on the edge.

"It's your fault, Violet. All of it. The guide died because of you. Ariel was hurt because of you. Jared died because of you. If you had just done what I wanted, no one would have been hurt. I hope that haunts you. I hope you spend the rest of our life knowing you could have saved everyone if you'd just been less selfish." He howled the last part, sidling closer to the edge.

Brayden was feet away, moving in from the left.

"You have a point," Gabe said, trying to buy time. "It's possible there will be charges pressed against Violet. For her part in all this."

"There should be. She has just as much responsibility as—"

Brayden yanked him down, rolling him onto his stomach and placing a knee in the small of his back. "You can finish that thought later. Right now, I'm going to read you your rights," he said.

He did so quickly, then dragged Lance upright and marched him out of the garage.

"That dude is delusional," Helena said, putting Luna back on her lead and giving her a treat. "Do you think he'd have really jumped?"

"No," Gabe said. He wasn't certain, but he thought Lance's sense of self-preservation was too high for him to take his own life.

"Maybe he would have," Violet said quietly. "That would have been the final word, you know? His way of placing the blame without giving me or anyone else a chance to state our side of the story."

Helena shook her head. "I, for one, am glad he's off the streets. All these months of searching, and we finally have our man. It's a good day's work, Gabe, and Bear did awesome! Maybe we should train him for suspect apprehension." She grinned.

"I think he'll stick to snow detection, but if there's ever a need for someone to be knocked to the ground, Bear's your dog." He scratched the St. Bernard's head, smiling when his tail thumped happily.

"I'll keep that in mind," Helena said. "I'm heading down. Do you want an ambulance for that gash?" she asked Violet.

"No. I'll just go to urgent care for stitches."

"I'll take you," Gabe offered.

"As long as it's not going to be a bother."

"Never," he replied gruffly.

"Hmm. Interesting." Helena smiled. "I'll leave you two to work out the details of that, and then I'll see you back at headquarters, Gabe." She walked off, Luna by her side.

"I meant what I said," Gabe said, taking off his jacket and dropping it around Violet's shoulders. "Helping you is never a bother."

"That's really sweet, but I've given you more than enough to do these past few weeks." A lump rose to her throat. "I'm sure you want to get back to a normal routine—"

"Is that what *you* want?" He took off his button-up

shirt, folded it and pressed it against the wound in her cheek.

"I thought I did. When I was in the Seavers' bunker, all I could think about was getting back home. Getting back to the life I'd built for myself after my parents died. Without Lance, of course. I was looking forward to being single. Raising Ava on my own. Being a strong, independent woman. I didn't plan to rely on anyone ever again. I didn't want to open my heart. It hurts too much to be fooled and used." She swiped at a tear, her hand trembling. This was an end for the K-9 team—closure on a case they'd been working for seven months.

But it was a beginning for Violet.

The very start of her healing. The very first day of her freedom from Lance and his control and manipulation.

"I understand," he said, tilting her chin so she was looking into his eyes. "And I'm not pressuring you for anything. Okay? The way I see things, you've got a fresh start, and you should do whatever you want with it."

"Can I be honest?" she whispered as he put her hand over the shirt and had her hold it in place.

"You know you can."

"The only future I can imagine is one with you in it. A fresh start and a new beginning will only make sense if you're part of them. You mended my broken heart, Gabe, and helped me believe in a dream I had stopped hoping for."

"Funny you should say that," he said, helping her to her feet. "Because I was thinking the same thing about my life. I've been a bachelor for a long time. It's time for something different, but only if that something different includes you."

"Just me?" she asked, and he could see a hint of anxiety in her eyes. She was a package deal.

That was fine.

He was, too.

"Of course not," he assured her. "You and Ava. And Bear, and any other kids and dogs and people we gather into our home."

"Be careful what you say. I've got a big house with lots of rooms to fill," she said with a laugh.

"True, but home isn't a house. It's a place in our hearts where the people we love live. When I'm with you and Ava, I'm there. You're deep in the part of my heart where no one else has ever lived. I love you both more than I ever imagine possible."

"I love you, too," she murmured, taking his hand, her fingers curving through his. "So, how about we go get Ava, get my stitches and get to work on our future?"

"That's the best idea I've heard in a while," he said, giving her a tender kiss, his heart beating hard for her, for Ava and for the life they'd have together.

"Come on, Bear," he called as they headed for the stairwell.

The K-9 lumbered after them, tail high, head proud.

He'd done an excellent job protecting a person he cared about, and he knew it.

It had been a tough journey to capture Lance, but the payoff was worth it. The team had closed another case, a killer was off the streets, and Gabe had found something he had never imagined was waiting for him.

Family.

Love.

Home.

All the things he had dreamed of as a child.

All the things he had stopped hoping for.

They were his, and he would never stop being grateful.

EPILOGUE

Thanksgiving Day

No pressure.

Just every one of the K-9 team members, their spouses or significant others, and their dogs, all gathered at the house for a feast and celebration that Violet was hosting.

She wasn't panicking. Not at all. Well, maybe a *little*. She wanted to do a good job. Not just for herself, but for Gabe.

Because his work comrades were his family.

She had grown to know and care about all of them while she was at the safe house. Now, two weeks later, after spending hours being interviewed about Lance and sharing the truth about their wildly toxic relationship, she felt she knew them all enough to know they wouldn't be judging her efforts here today.

Still, she wanted Gabe to be happy.

She supposed that was part of being in love with someone who loved her back. In fact, Gabe had helped her plan the whole event. He'd bought the turkeys, helped her choose a menu, and he had even offered to take care of Ava while she was getting the house ready. And while Violet certainly could have catered everything—could have hired people to do all the work—she knew her mother and father had felt that preparing for guests was part of extending hospitality.

So, other than asking the housekeeper to help make certain the turkey didn't overcook and the appetizers were ready on time, she'd done all the work herself.

Not an easy job with an infant around.

"But I don't mind, love. You're worth it," she told Ava, lifting her out of the baby swing and kissing her chubby cheek. "What do you think? Nice?" She spun around to face the table with the bright white china and flower centerpieces.

Ava cooed.

"I thought you would. The guests should be here soon. Hopefully Gabe will arrive first. I want to make sure he's happy with everything."

As if any of it mattered to him.

He would have been content to host the Thanksgiving feast at the office. In fact, he'd even suggested setting up tables in the conference room, because he hadn't wanted to put pressure on her. Gabe had been worried about how the investigation and the looming trial were affecting her.

Sometimes she woke up in a cold sweat, reliving those moments in the parking garage, hearing Lance's taunting words.

She'd always call Gabe, and he always answered.

He'd talk her through the bad moments, help her reason through her fear, and he'd encouraged her to focus on other things.

Violet had been turning her attention to her father's business and to helping the medical clinic. She had visited them two days ago and gone over plans to expand the facility.

She owed a lot of people, and she planned to repay them.

To that end, she had already offered Harrison funds for college. She was prepping a room over the garage—his own place where he could be free to come and go but still have all the modern conveniences he craved. He was incredibly grateful to her, thanking her repeatedly even though she'd told him there was no need, and she smiled when she recalled how touched he'd been when he learned she had invited his entire family to her Thanksgiving banquet.

Though she had no idea if all the Seavers were coming.

Eli still hadn't heard from Cole, and Bettina was getting sicker every day.

Life was fragile.

Time was fleeting.

Violet was sorry that a man she respected couldn't see that he was squandering both.

The doorbell rang, and she hurried to answer it, glancing out the peephole, her heart swelling when she saw Gabe and Bear.

If love were a photograph, it would be blue sky and white clouds, snow-capped mountains and a cabin in the woods. It would be this man and his dog, stepping into the foyer, Gabe in a suit, Bear wearing a bow tie.

They took her breath away.

"You two are looking very handsome," she said,

standing on her toes to steal a kiss. She had never loved anyone the way she loved Gabe. Freely and without self-consciousness. This man had seen her at her worst, and he had never judged her for it. He knew her secrets and her scars, and he loved her anyway.

"And you both look beautiful," he murmured against her lips, his hands sliding down her back and settling at the curve of her waist. "Did you eat today?"

"You ask me that every time you see me," she said with a laugh, stepping back but not going far. She liked being close. Knowing that he was there. A best friend, a companion, a partner.

"Because you forget every time I don't see you," he chided.

"I had toast. Danielle made it for me while I was putting the turkeys in the oven." Danielle had been her parents' housekeeper for a decade before their deaths. She'd continued to work for Violet, but they were more friends than employee and employer.

"I guess the bribe to keep you fed paid off," he said.

"You did *not* pay her to get me to eat," she responded with a laugh, leading the way into the dining room, the scents of turkey and dressing filling the air.

"Okay, you're right. I didn't, but I thought about it. I worry for you, Violet. It's not just you you're nourishing." He touched her chin, kissed her forehead.

"I know. I'm doing better. It's just been so busy since I've returned. Once the banquet is over, things will be calmer."

"And then you'll be prepping for some big Christmas shindig," he commented, his lips quirking in a half smile.

"Would you mind?"

"What makes you happy makes me happy," he responded. "Besides, I never had big gatherings when I was a kid. No family to gather, so this is nice." He walked to the table, lifting one of the placeholders she'd made. "This is amazing, Violet. You're amazing."

"I learned from my parents. They were fabulous hosts."

The doorbell rang, and her heart jumped.

"This is it! The first guest is here," she said, breathless with sudden anxiety and nerves. What if the turkey was dry? What if the veggies were tasteless? What if she gave everyone food poisoning?

"Honey, don't look like the world is about to end, okay? Everyone coming today cares about you. Not the food or the table or the flowers. Just you." Gabe kissed her deeply, passionately, wiping away all thoughts of dry turkey or dissatisfied guests.

Bear gave a quiet woof, and they broke apart, breathless staring into each other's eyes.

"If you were trying to distract me, it worked," she said.

"Good, because here comes Eli, and from what I hear, he can eat!"

"I have enough to feed a small army," she said, her cheeks warm with excitement and nerves.

The rest of the team arrived in pairs.

Hunter and Ariel with Juneau and Ariel's young husky, Sasha.

Poppy and her new husband, Lex, and his toddler son. They'd married right after the case wrapped up. Stormy loped in beside the happy newlyweds and made herself at home near the fireplace.

Maya and her significant other, David, arrived next,

Sarge prancing in front of them, eager to play with his canine friends.

It wasn't long before the hearth room was filled with people—Helena and her fiancé, Everett, Luna standing protectively between them. Will and his beloved bride-to-be, Jasmine. Their dog, Scout, playing happily with Bear. Sean and Ivy West with their son, Grace lying near the little boy's feet. Brayden and his fiancée, Katie Kapowski. Katie was the assistant to Colonel Lorenza Gallo, who stood in the center of the room, petting Brayden's dog, Ella.

Violet's housekeeper, Danielle, was standing near the doorway, dressed in a beautiful pink sheath. Violet had wanted her to attend. Not just to help with the banquet. She was family, and Violet wanted her to know it.

"It looks like everyone is here," she called above the chatter. "The food is ready, so how about we go ahead and say grace? Then we'll go into the dining room to eat. We're doing buffet style. Danielle and I have already set everything out. Gabe has offered to pray."

Gabe's prayer was heartfelt and sincere, filled with thanksgiving for all God had brought to the team. The relationships. The friendships. The solved cases.

When he finished, the group moved to the dining room, gathering around tables laden with food.

"A feast fit for a family," Gabe whispered in Violet's ear.

"You haven't tasted it yet. You might say something different once you do," she responded playfully.

He, more than any other person she knew, could make her heart sing. Not with joy or passion. Although she felt those things, too. With contentment.

He was the right fit. The puzzle piece sliding right into place.

As everyone took their seats, the doorbell rang.

Surprised, Violet hurried to the door, Gabe right beside her.

She glanced through the peephole and was shocked to see the Seavers standing on her porch.

She fumbled with the doorknob, yanked the door open and dragged Dana Seaver into her arms, Ava sandwiched between them. "You came!" she cried.

"We wouldn't have missed it. I'm sorry we are late. It's a bit of a trip out here, and we had to hire a car to bring us." Dana glanced at her husband and son. "We also didn't have suits or dresses or anything. I mean, this is kind of a fancy place. If you'd rather us not come in…"

"Don't be silly! You're dressed perfectly." She stepped back, ushering them into her house and seeing it through their eyes. The gleaming floors and bright lights. The excess.

"I can take your coats," Gabe offered. "I'm Gabriel Runyon. Violet's friend."

He hung their coats in the closet, making small talk and doing everything he could to put them at ease.

Violet appreciated that about him.

The way he strove to make everyone feel accepted and valued. Watching him made her heart go soft and her eyes misty.

"Friend, huh?" Harrison whispered as they walked into the dining room.

"*Good* friend," she corrected.

He laughed.

The boisterous conversation quieted as the Seavers

approached, everyone offering smiles and hellos to the newcomers.

"Everyone, these are—"

"Cole?" Eli jumped up, obviously surprised to see his godmother's son.

"That's right," Cole said. "And you're Eli. I'm surprised you remember me. It's been a while."

"A while? That's an understatement. How have you been?" Eli pulled the other man in for a bear hug.

"Good, but I hear things aren't as good for my mother. I don't want to steal any joy from the day, and I don't want the meal to be about us, but I wanted you to know, I've thought about what Violet said in her letter. She's right. Life is too precious to waste it on old hurt feelings and grudges. Mom made mistakes, but I did, too. After the meal, I'd like to go see her. If you wouldn't mind taking me."

"*Mind!* I'm going to text and tell her that you're coming. She's going to be overjoyed. Thank you, Cole! You don't know how much this means to her and to me."

"How is she? Violet said she's in hospice." Cole took the seat beside Eli.

"She is, but she's started an experimental treatment, and the tumors have shrunk. The doctor thinks we've bought some time."

"I'm grateful," Cole murmured. "I've been praying that I'd have time to make up for what we missed out on. My family and I are going to get a place close by. As Violet might have already told you, Harrison wants to attend college, and Dana doesn't want to be out off the grid and out of touch anymore. She's a good mom, and I won't make her give up her relationship with our child for my ideologies. Plus, ideologics change, and I've realized we've missed out on a lot."

"Cole, do you mean it," Dana asked, her eyes welling with tears. "We're moving back to town?"

"I mean it, sweetheart. I know you haven't been happy since Violet left, and you're going to be miserable with Harrison gone."

"But what about you? I don't want you to be unhappy," Dana said.

"How can I be if I'm with you?"

"Please, guys. No mushy stuff," Harrison griped, but it was obvious he was touched by his parents' love for one another.

Violet was, too.

How could she not be?

She nibbled on turkey and listened to the conversation swirl around her. A houseful of people who cared so much for each other, and she felt blessed and privileged to be part of their world.

The doorbell rang again as everyone gathered in the hearth room for coffee, tea and dessert.

Violet rose from her spot near the piano, but Gabe put his hand on her arm.

"I'll get it. You look tired."

"I'm content," she corrected, touching his knuckles. "But I'll let you get the door. Thank you."

He walked away, returning moments later with a large box in his hand.

The room went silent, everyone suddenly focused on Gabe.

"What's that?" Violet asked, getting up from her seat,

worried that something was wrong. That maybe Lance had managed to send a bomb from prison.

"A surprise the team and I have been working on," he responded.

"Here, let me take the little one," Danielle said, hurrying over and lifting Ava from Violet's arms.

"Were you in on the surprise, too?" she asked.

Danielle grinned. "Of course!"

Gabe set the box on the floor.

It moved. Shimmying to the left and surprising a squeal out of Violet.

"Gabe! What have you done?" she asked, kneeling in front of the box.

"Open it and see," he said with a self-satisfied smile. "Just remember, we did discuss how much room you have here."

"I remember." She lifted the lid off, looked into the box and saw a fuzzy face peering up at her.

Brown and white. Floppy ears. Broad head.

A St. Bernard puppy!

"Gabe!" she cried. "She's perfect!"

"He. Bear wanted a brother," he said with a laugh, leaning down to kiss her head as she lifted the wiggling puppy from the box.

"*He* is perfect!" she said, laughing when the puppy licked her face. "What's his name?"

"Check his tag," he suggested, grinning broadly.

She reached under his soft fur, found the tag and leaned close to read it. "Will?" she asked. "I'd have thought you'd be a little more creative."

"Turn it over," he urged.

She flipped the tag, her heart skipping a beat when she saw the words engraved there: *you marry me?*

"Gabe!" She jumped to her feet, nearly knocking him over as she threw herself into his arms. "You know I will."

"When?" he asked, kissing her gently. Tenderly. As if they were the only two people in the room.

"You pick the day," she said, meaning every word. "I'll be there."

"Then I choose today."

The words hung in the silence, frozen in the beauty of the perfect gift and the perfect proposal given by a man who was absolutely perfect for her.

He was waiting for her response, his body relaxed, his jaw tense. It had taken a lot for him to do this. To put his love out there for everyone to see. He had been hurt as a child, yet somehow, he had still grown into a man who could give of himself. And right now he was putting it all on the line for her, risking the ultimate rejection. Not just in a private setting…but in front of the people he respected most.

She loved him even more for that.

"We need to find a pastor," she said, and she could see tension slide from his face, see joy fill his eyes.

"I have good news for you," Lorenza said. "I just happened to be ordained. I also just happened to have a marriage license with me."

"Just *happened* to, huh?" she said, looking into Gabe's eyes.

"Absolutely," he responded, taking her hands. "So, how about it? Want to get hitched?"

"Absolutely," she responded.

And so they did, standing in front of the people who cared about them both, repeating vows to one another, promising to cherish and to love, to honor and to respect.

The fire crackled in the hearth.

The puppy played at their feet, the canine members of the team watching with interest as Will rolled onto his back and snuffled Violet's shoes.

Snow began to fall, drifting outside the window in fat white flakes that would soon paint the world in wintry light. Danielle stood nearby, Ava in her arms, tears of happiness sliding down her cheeks.

Violet noticed those things, but more than everything else, she noticed the love in Gabe's eyes, the sincerity in his words. His hands were warm as he cupped her cheeks and kissed her to seal their vows.

Their friends cheered and Will howled, startled by the cacophony of noise. Bear walked over and nudged him, urging him to play.

And Violet had never felt so content.

She had never felt so at home.

This was what she had longed for when she had met Lance. If she could go back and rewrite her story, she wouldn't edit out the chapter that had brought her to this place.

As hard as it had been, as challenging as she had found it, it had brought her Ava and Gabe, Bear and Will. It had brought her a network of friends she could count on for support. It had brought her passion and focus and a desire to help more, do more, contribute more.

It had renewed her faith, it had strengthened her and, most of all, it had brought her home.

To this place in Gabe's arms.

"I love you, sweetheart," he whispered against her lips. "Always and forever."

"I love you, too," she replied, sliding her hands through his hair and kissing him deeply while the fire crackled and the snow fell and the people they loved cheered them on.

* * * * *

Alaska K-9 Unit
These state troopers fight for justice
with the help of their brave canine partners.

Dear Reader,

I've spent the past two and a half years training to be part of Chesapeake Search Dogs, an all-volunteer non-profit organization dedicated to finding the lost and missing and bringing them home. My work with the group and with my search dog, Huxley, has helped me appreciate even more the incredible partnership between K-9 handlers and their canine partners. It was an honor and privilege to tie up the Alaskan K-9 Unit series. I hope you enjoyed reading the wilderness adventures as much as I enjoyed writing about them!

I love connecting with readers. You can find me on Facebook or Instagram or drop me a line at shirleermccoy@hotmail.com.

Blessings,
Shirlee